THE FAIRY GARDEN

by Diana Nokaj

For more information, contact:

(diananokaj90@gmail.com)

THE FAIRY GARDEN

To the girl who once believed in fairy tales,

You didn't know how, but you always knew why.

Thank you for writing this story.

CONTENTS

Do You Believe in Fairy Tales?

CHAPTER 1

WHO ARE YOU?

Somewhere far beyond, a voice called out my name. "Victoria... Victoria!" I was afraid. Never before had I heard such a voice. It echoed from afar, relentless in its call. In the depth of the shadows, I stood there—alone with my silence—until a voice, soft and strange, whispered my name so beautifully. I am lost, wandering upon a dark and endless sea. And there it is again... that peculiar voice, haunting my dreams, never showing its face. I don't know who calls, for no answer comes in return. "Who calls me? Who are you?" I opened my eyes and turned to my left. There sat Papa, quietly reading a book. For a moment, I had quite forgotten our long journey. In truth, we had been travelling for several days, making our way to a more peaceful place. Our new home lay somewhere in the countryside near Dorchester. The journey was long and, to me, rather tiresome. Papa finished his reading and looked at me with a tender smile. "Good morning, Victoria."

My name is Victoria Erin Flynn, and I am twelve years old. I was named in honour of Her Majesty, Queen Victoria, and after my dear grandmother, Erin. I was born in London, on the twelfth of October, in 1842. My papa's name is Adam Flynn, and he is thirty-four. He is a writer and playwright. Though not particularly tall, he is fairly handsome, light brown hair with piercing blue eyes, which I am proud to say I have inherited. He is, in every sense, a gentleman and noble in spirit. He finds his greatest joy in books, particularly the works of William Shakespeare, whom he deeply admires. Papa is of Irish descent. His father, Simon David Flynn, was a well-regarded architect, while his mother, Erin Flynn (née Doyle), was a poet in her quiet way. They had two sons—my father, Adam, and his younger brother, David. My grandparents passed away when Papa was still very young. Though I never had the pleasure of knowing them, I've come to know their kindness and warmth through Papa's many stories. As for my uncle David, I know little of him. He departed for France at the age of fifteen and never returned. From time to time, he sends letters from Paris, where he resides with his wife and their two daughters. Papa always receives these letters with quiet joy, and though he rarely speaks of his brother, there is a fondness in his eyes when he does. After a long and tiring journey, we arrived at our new home at last. Yet, I wasn't pleased—for I missed my home in London. Still, I was left with no choice but to follow my papa, who had, quite without warning, decided to move to the village where his grandfather had once resided. We were to live in the very house that had belonged to him. Oh, how I shall miss my beloved home—but most of all, my beautiful garden, where I spent most of my hours tending the flowers. It was my mother's garden… My dear Mama! She passed when I was only six—far too young to fathom what death truly meant. Her passing was a sudden mystery, and when she left us, she took with her the greater part of my joy. I dream of her still, almost every night—her kind face radiant as moonlight, her sweet and delicate smile, her scent of roses. But when I run to embrace her, I cannot reach her… for it is only a dream—A passing image. And so, I have come to dread my dreams.

…

"Look, Victoria! Isn't it beautiful, my dear?" Adam gestured toward the house—their new home. An elegant Georgian manor, full of charm and grace, like something out of a fairy tale. Covered in ivy like a green blanket and blooming red roses, the house had once belonged to Adam's grandfather. Now, as the rightful heir of the Flynn family, it was his.

"What do you think?" asked Adam.

Victoria shrugged her shoulders, "I don't know."

"From this day forth, this shall be our home."

"I don't like it here!" Victoria trembled, shadowed by a quiet melancholy. Tears began to fall silently down her cheeks. Adam, startled by her sudden shift in her mood, reached into his pocket, withdrew a handkerchief, and gently wiped her tears. "It's all right, darling."

At that moment, a tall, older gentleman appeared upon the front steps. Nearly sixty, with a white beard and striking green eyes. With a warm smile, he greeted them. "Welcome home, sir!"

Victoria gazed at him with curiosity and caution, then turned to her father. "Who is that man, Papa?"

"That is Thomas," answered Adam. "He has looked after the house for as long as anyone can recall."

The gentleman bowed courteously and introduced himself with grace: "Thomas Green, at your service. You must be little Victoria. What a pleasure to make your acquaintance at last, miss."

Thomas Green—he had, in truth, spent nearly all his life serving faithfully within those walls. There was something peculiar about him that immediately drew Victoria's attention.

"Thomas's father was my grandfather's butler," Adam explained. "Would you be so kind as to assist us with the luggage, Thomas?"

"Yes, sir! Right away, sir!... Henryyy!"

Suddenly, from out of nowhere, came a fourteen-year-old boy wearing a brown flat cap that shadowed his green eyes and auburn hair. His name was Henry. "Welcome, sir!" he took off his hat and gave a shy bow.

"Thank you, Henry," Adam replied warmly. "My word! You've become quite the young man, indeed."

Henry blushed, then quickly moved to gather the suitcases and carry them inside.

Meanwhile, Victoria felt a wave of uncertainty. She could never have imagined that her father knew all these people, he had never once spoken of them.

Turning to her with a kind smile, Adam said: "Come along, dear. Let us enter our new home."

As they passed through the door, the household staff stood in a respectful line to receive them. Alongside Thomas were two housemaids; Ruth and Isabelle—and Henry, the young gardener. They all welcomed the new owners with warmth and respect, as custom required. Victoria glanced at Henry, thinking to herself, "*He's just a boy.*"

"Isabelle," Adam called. "Would you be so kind as to show Victoria to her room?"

When Victoria stepped into her new bedroom for the first time, she was amazed by how much it resembled the one she had left behind in London. It was no coincidence—Adam had ensured all was arranged to her liking, so she wouldn't miss her old belongings.

"I pray this is to your liking, miss," said Isabelle. Victoria did not respond. Her eyes wandered across the room until they settled upon a white balcony. Without a word, she asked Isabelle to leave her. She wished to be alone. She rested her head on the pillow, as the long journey had left her drained. As she closed her eyes, a single tear slipped down her cheek—quiet as a raindrop falling from a grey sky. It was a moment of despair; sinking further into melancholy. How many times had she promised her father she would no longer cry? Yet her tears betrayed her, again and again. Victoria looked like an angel—with golden hair, eyes the colour of the summer sky, skin pale and delicate, and a scent like that of a rose garden. A fragile angel, yes—but one with a broken heart and broken wings.

"*Mama... Mama, why did you leave me?*" she cried. "*You said we'd always be together.*" Exhaustion pulled her under as she drifted into sleep with the word *Always* on her lips.

"*Victoria... Victoria... wake up!*"

The voice returned—soft, distant, and haunting. "*Who are you?*" she demanded. "*Why do you haunt me? Why do you call my name?*"

Adam sat quietly beside her bed, watching as she slept profoundly. He gently kissed her forehead and whispered, "Sweet dreams, my fairy."

But Victoria feared sleep. Sleep was the gateway to dreams. And dreams, for her, were no harmless illusions. Those dreams had become nightmares. Night after night, the same dream. Distant whispers, voices calling her name but never showing their face. More than anything, she wished to see her mother again. To feel her arms around her. To say all the things that had been left unsaid. Dreams were the only place where such a reunion could exist—where love could defy death, if only for a moment. For in dreams, her mother still lived. And Victoria feared the day she could no longer remember her face. For when a person dies, their story dies with them. And they can be easily forgotten. These are the so-called *Dreams*, and it is no simple thing to explain them.

CHAPTER 2

ALL THAT GLITTERS IS NOT GOLD

After a long night, a new day dawned. Morning sunlight pierced through the curtains, and from the open windows came the sweet chirping of birds. It was summertime. The village scenery was truly picturesque, rich with pure, unspoiled nature. In summer, the days were long and mild, though rain was never far behind. Endless green fields, and the summer breeze carried the soft scent of roses.

"Are you awake, miss?" Isabelle knocked on the door. Victoria slowly opened her eyes and realized she wasn't in her old bedroom. Upon hearing the loud knocks, she got angry and spoke in a louder tone: "What do you want?"

At times, she could be quite impolite. Spoiled outrageously by her doting father.

"...Begging your pardon, miss... your father requests you join him for breakfast."

"Very well—tell him I shall be down shortly."

Victoria had slept wonderfully; more soundly than she had in many weeks. After washing her face and brushing her teeth, she wore a blue dress and brown leather shoes. She combed her hair, then made her way down the staircase. In the dining room, her father sat at the head of the table, and Thomas was standing on his left.

"Ah—good morning, my dear," Adam said warmly. "I trust you slept well?"

Victoria felt a little shy around Thomas, as he was still unfamiliar to her. Then, she placed the napkin upon her lap and began eating with the elegance of a well-raised young lady. As they ate, Adam set down his fork and said: "I was thinking... we might attend the church service this evening."

"I'd rather not."

"But why, my darling?"

"I don't feel like going anywhere."

"Oh, Victoria... you mustn't do this to yourself," Adam said sadly. "Loneliness, my dear, is a cruel companion."

"Perhaps not."

"You sound just like David..."

"What of him?"

"At times, you remind me of my brother. He, too, was often low in spirits. It pains me to see you like this, my darling. Will you smile for me?"

She pretended not to hear, but her trembling hands betrayed her, and the spoon slipped from her fingers.

"Is something the matter, Victoria?"

"It is nothing, Papa," she replied with a trembling voice.

"Are you feeling unwell?"

"I... I don't know. It's just that—"

And for a moment, she lost consciousness—Then collapsed from her chair. Adam tried to catch her, but she slipped from his grasp and fell to the floor.

"Victoria, Victoria!" he called out desperately. "Thomas! Quick—help me!"

They carefully laid her down on the couch; her skin was flushed with fever, and she was barely able to breathe. Moments later, Dr. Griffiths, the village physician, arrived.

"Is it the summer cold?" Adam asked anxiously.

"Certainly not! You needn't worry."

"Then what is it, doctor?"

The doctor looked at him steadily. "Has anything like this occurred before?"

"I think not."

"Then it is clear," Dr. Griffiths sighed.

"What is clear?"

"Your daughter is not ill—she longs for the comfort of home. What she requires is rest. With time, she will adjust. I strongly advise you not to put her under undue pressure."

"Good heavens, doctor—I would never do such a thing!"

"You must remember, she is but a child, and it will require time for her to accustom herself to such a sudden change. I trust I've made myself clear, have I not, sir?" the doctor said, with a mild reproach.

"Yes, yes—most certainly. Thank you, doctor," replied the confused Adam.

Thomas escorted Dr. Griffiths out, while Adam remained at his daughter's side, stroking her hair with quiet tenderness. "All shall be well." he whispered.

As the front door shut, Henry slowly approached Thomas to ask about Victoria.

"How is she? Is she any better?"

"It's no business of yours. Return to your duties at once!" he responded harshly. The boy looked at him fiercely and muttered to himself, *"Bloody old man!"*

Thomas observed silently as Adam worried himself sick; He pretended not to comprehend a father's love. Then he slowly stepped forward to ask if he needed anything. Before he withdrew, Adam's voice stopped him. "Do you have children, Thomas?"

Thomas froze. He shut his eyes in anguish and took a deep breath. "No, sir... I do not."

"Strange, isn't it?" replied Adam. "Your answer lacks conviction."

"I... I had a son, sir... He is no longer with us," he admitted at last. Adam turned his head, shaken by the confession. "I'm sorry to hear that. May I ask — what happened to him?"

"I would rather not speak of it, if you don't mind, sir."

"Of course. I didn't mean to upset you... That will be all."

"With your permission, sir," Thomas replied and withdrew quietly.

"Goodness," thought Adam as he gazed at Victoria's

angelic face. He remembered how cheerful she once was, when her mother still walked the earth. With every step, Victoria was at her side, never letting go of her hand. "My dearest... Avelina," he sighed painfully. "Life without you seems to hold no meaning."

Adam had been deeply in love with his wife. Even now, he found it almost impossible to accept that she was truly gone. And yet, her presence lingered in every corner—like a wandering spirit, quietly watching over them.

...

In the afternoon, the household was occupied with its chores. Adam was writing in his study. A heavy silence prevailed; one could only hear the steady tick of the pendulum clock. Victoria was still asleep, and her father was worried that she might be falling ill. He wasn't in the mood to write—his thoughts kept drifting to his daughter's well-being. Thomas entered the room carrying a tray.

"Your tea, sir."

"Thank you, Thomas."

"You seem troubled."

"How could I not be? I am utterly worried."

14

"Do not worry, sir. You heard what the doctor said—her condition is not very serious."

"I pray he's right."

Adam longed for companionship—someone to confide in, someone to whom he could open his heart. Though he was not accustomed to speaking so openly with servants, Thomas was something of an exception. He regarded him as a trusted friend of the family. Besides, Adam was a kind man.

"You know, Thomas... Victoria was once full of spirit. The day she was born was the happiest of my life. I wept like a child, I truly did. Avelina and I—" he paused for a moment.

"Avelina?"

"Yes. My late wife," he smiled sadly and spoke of her with the most delightful words. "She was the most beautiful woman I had ever known, Thomas. She seemed fairy-like, her eyes shimmered like starlight, and her voice... was like music to my ears."

"Do you know the meaning of her name?" asked Thomas, quite unexpectedly.

He shook his head slowly, "I think not."

"Avelina—it sounds very much like the name of a fairy."

"And how do you know this?"

"The myths of the fairies have always intrigued me."

"If such creatures exist, then surely they must be beautiful," said Adam.

Thomas smirked and replied with a touch of irony, "All that glitters is not gold, sir."

CHAPTER 3

THE SECRET DOOR

Three days had gone by, and Victoria was confined to her room by choice. Though Adam had made every effort to lift her spirits, she could barely know the cause of her melancholy. He blamed himself, compelling her to adjust to a new life. She was lying in bed when he entered her room.

"Come, my dear. Let us take a walk. The country air shall do you good."

She did not say a word; instead, she turned away and remained silent.

"Have I upset you? Talk to me, Victoria—I beg you, do not ignore me," Adam said with sad eyes.

She was not truly angry with him, only overcome by a strange and sudden melancholy she could not explain.

"I... I..."

"Speak, dear."

"I love you dearly, Papa," she began to sob.

Adam folded her into his arms. "Oh, my sweetheart, you know I love you more than life itself."

In truth, he had no one in the world but her. The two of them remained in each other's arms for a while. "You must not frighten me so again, do you hear?"

"Forgive me, Papa. I can't explain myself, I'm afraid…"

"It's all right. Now, dry your eyes and come with me."

"Where are we going, Papa?"

"I have a surprise for you."

Victoria fancied surprises, though she did not offer a smile. Eager and curious about her father's surprise, she came downstairs to find Adam waiting for her. "Come," he said, extending his hand. And so, hand in hand she followed his light steps, unaware of what was ahead of her.

"A kitten, perhaps? Or a little puppy? Or just a plain new doll?" she thought to herself.

They walked through a small passage that led to an old wooden door. It was unlike the others—unique and mysterious. But what lay beyond that secret door? She was soon to find out.

"Where are we going, Papa?" she asked again.

"Patience, my dear," he smiled. "We are nearly there."

"What's behind the door? Is this your surprise?"

"Open it!" he said at last.

She opened the secret door slowly. For a moment, she remained still, breathless, unable to speak. She could not believe her eyes. Surely, this had to be a dream—it was far too perfect to be real. Before her, something out of a fairytale. The door led right into the most enchanted garden she had ever seen. Vast and full of blooming flowers of every color, shape, and scent. Yet it was more than a garden. No—this place resembled an ancient woodland, where nature's most magical creatures might dwell.

"Am I in heaven?" she whispered. "Papa... it looks like the Garden of Eden."

Victoria stepped into the garden alongside her father, breathing in the flowers that surrounded her. How she adored flowers—always had. And yet, her father did not even see a trace of joy on her face. *"I sort of hoped she'd smile again,"* he thought.

"Papa, look over there!"

Adam turned and saw a bird's nest. Chuckling softly, he said: "It seems we are not the only ones who have made a home here."

...

"Have you heard? Miss Victoria has finally stepped out of her room!" Isabelle whispered to Ruth.

"What of it, Isabelle?"

"What do you mean? The poor girl's been shut away for days."

Ruth set down her spoon when she addressed her with an irritating tone: "Will you stop that nonsense? Leave the girl alone and mind your own business!"

Just then, Henry stepped in and reached for the food, but Ruth smacked his hand with a wooden spoon. "Don't you dare!"

"But I'm hungry," the boy complained.

"These are not for you! I'll fetch you something else."

Isabelle was a twenty-year-old and a chatterbox; she talked a lot, even when scolded. As soon as Ruth stepped away, she seized her chance. "Henry..."

"What, Isabelle?"

"Miss Victoria came out of her room."

"What now?"

"I'm saying—she came out."

"Are you sure?"

"Of course! She's in the garden with her father."

"In the garden?"

Before Isabelle could say another word, Ruth returned and scolded her once more. "Insolent girl! That's quite enough!"

"But Ruth, I was only—"

"I'll hear no more of it, understood?"

"All right—I'm leaving!" Isabelle hurried away.

"What is it, Mother?"

"She's insufferable, that one!"

"Pay her no mind, you know how she is."

"I know, I know! Now finish your supper. I've got chores to do."

Yes, you heard that right—Ruth is Henry's mother. A short while later, Thomas entered the kitchen, saw Henry eating, and addressed him with a sharp tone. "What are you still doing here? Shouldn't you be in the garden?"

"I... I was hungry—" the boy stammered.

"Make haste. There's work to be done." Thomas demanded after attacking the poor boy for no apparent reason. Henry clenched his spoon tightly and whispered, "I loathe you."

His mother noticed an indescribable hatred in his eyes. Then she spoke to him softly: "No, Henry. You mustn't. He is—"

"I don't much care who he is," Henry said.

...

Victoria had spent quite some time in the enchanting garden. Seated upon a wooden bench, she was feeding the birds with her small hand. Henry spotted her from a distance. At first, he was too shy to speak, but curiosity got the better of him, and he stepped closer.

"Are you fond of birds?" he asked.

She lifted her head at the sound of his voice. She was stunned, for it was the first time he had spoken to her. Never before had they exchanged a word.

"I beg your pardon?" she replied.

"I said... are... you... fond... of birds?" he repeated with a silly tone. Uncertain how to address a lady.

"What sort of a question is that?"

"Oh, my! You are rather rude!" he said with a teasing smile.

She lowered her eyes, suddenly embarrassed.

Without another word, she rose and fled swiftly. Henry was taken aback by her sudden retreat. *"What a peculiar girl,"* he thought to himself.

Victoria hurried to her room and shut the door behind her. With a sigh of relief, she muttered: "Silly fool! Who does he think he is?"

Leaning against the door, she took a few steps before moving to the balcony. As she drew the curtain aside, she saw Henry tending the garden below. The boy who had dared to tease her. At that moment, Isabelle entered, carrying a small tray.

"Miss," she called. "I brought you something to eat."

Victoria told her to leave. "I need nothing. You may go."

"As you wish, miss." Just as Isabelle made her way to the door, Victoria stopped her with a question.

"Wait! What is that boy doing in our garden?"

"Oh, you mean Henry? He's our gardener."

"The gardener?" Victoria repeated.

"Indeed. Thanks to his care, the garden looks wonderful. You've seen it, haven't you?"

"Does that mean he tends to everything? The flowers... the birds...?"

"Yes, yes... of course. He's quite the charming

fellow, wouldn't you agree, miss?" Isabelle teased lightly.

Victoria blushed at her bold question. After a long pause, she exclaimed, "How dare you? You insult me by talking such nonsense!"

Isabelle, realizing she had overstepped, bowed her head in apology. "I'm sorry, miss. I talk too much. Please forgive me, miss."

Little Victoria had grown to love that enchanted garden, yet refused to acknowledge that it was Henry who had tended it with such tenderness. "*That can't be,*" she thought, gazing down once more. Then she whispered absentmindedly: "I wish to be part of that garden... to live there forever."

If only she knew how perilous the demands of the heart can be. Wishes, once granted, come at a price. Wishes that may turn to regret. Be careful what you wish for!

CHAPTER 4

DO YOU BELIEVE IN FAIRY TALES?

"Was it only a dream? If it truly was a dream, then it was the most beautiful dream I have ever dreamed. No… I can't get it out of my head. Where am I now? I can feel it… I can hear it… and I will find it. I will claim it and never let it go. What is this strange feeling? Where does it come from? Is it mine alone?"

"Come…Victoria…"

"There it is again—the voice, rising from the shadows. Now I can hear it better. A divine voice. I can't say from where it calls, but it sounds like the sweetest music. I must follow it—it calls my name. Though unknown to me, it is beautiful. There! It calls again. I must go… I must…"

"Wake up, Victoria!"

"Papa?"

"What is it? You were talking in your sleep."

"Papa, where am I?"

"Why, in your bed, my dear!"

"What time is it?"

"It is morning. Come now, get dressed—we are going for a stroll after breakfast."

"Papa!"

"Yes, darling?"

"I was there."

"Where?"

"I saw Heaven... but Mama was not there."

"It was only a dream, child."

"No, it was more than a dream. I was there—and someone was calling my name."

"Victoria, my dear. Dreams are not reality."

"You don't believe me... do you?"

He kissed her on the forehead and left, having nothing further to say. Victoria did not feel well, yet she kept her discomfort to herself. Saddened by the fact that her father had not taken her words seriously.

"Thomas!" called Adam. "Ready the carriage—we are going for a stroll."

"Yes, sir. I shall have it ready at once."

Victoria went out silently and into the carriage with a gloomy face. She remained quiet throughout the ride, while Adam flipped through pages of a small book. He glanced over at her, who sat thoughtfully and disheartened.

"Do you remember," he began, "when you were little and insisted upon sleeping in the garden? Your mother and I tried to persuade you otherwise, but you would say, '*I wish to stay here forever,*'... '*This is my paradise,*'... '*A voice is calling me*'... You were such a little dreamer. I worried a lot, and your mother merely laughed, '*Let her dream.*' she would say."

For a brief moment, Victoria felt a deep longing and wiped her teary eyes.

"Forgive me—I didn't mean to," said Adam softly.

"Do not worry, Papa." She paused, then turned the conversation elsewhere. Her mind was intrigued by the young gardener named Henry.

"What is the name of the boy who tends the garden?"

"Who—Henry? Do you not remember his name?"

"I do not," she lied.

"Henry is Ruth's son."

"Really?"

"Indeed."

"How old is he?"

"Fourteen—perhaps fifteen. I cannot say with certainty."

Then she let out a quiet sigh.

"Is something the matter, my darling?"

"I don't want to grow older. I wish I could remain a child... forever," she said so suddenly.

Adam laughed wholeheartedly; her words had the power to move him—sometimes to laughter, other times to tears.

...

After a pleasant stroll through the countryside, they returned home late in the evening. Thomas was waiting for them at the gate, holding an envelope.

"What news have you, Thomas?"

"A letter arrived this afternoon for you, sir. It is from London."

"Let me see." Adam broke the seal and, after reading the note, turned to Victoria. "It appears I must return to London for a few days!"

"I thought you said we were to stay here from now on. You said so yourself..."

"It is but a matter of days. They require my presence at the theatre."

"Then take me with you!"

"Victoria, dearest!" he interrupted gently. "You must stay here, with Thomas and the others."

"Please, Papa!" she pleaded.

"I'd love to take you... but I'll be occupied at the theatre most of the time, and it is hardly a proper place for a child."

"Papa, do not leave me alone."

"You won't be alone, dear," Adam glanced toward Thomas. "I shall depart first thing in the morning, all right?"

"All right, Papa," she agreed through tears.

It was midnight, and all were profoundly asleep, except Victoria. For the first time, her father was leaving her in the company of strangers. Everything about that place felt strange and foreign. *Now, what am I to do without my Papa?* A hundred questions wandered through her mind. As her thoughts grew heavy, she slowly closed her eyes, for sleep was approaching. Ready to sail upon the sea of dreams, she was suddenly awakened by a familiar voice. *"Wake up, Victoria!"* There was no one in the room. The moonlight streamed through the windows, its silver glow softening the midnight shadows. Weary as she was, the voice no longer startled her, and she flew once more into the realm of dreams.

....

The next morning, Adam departed for London, having instructed everyone to keep a close eye on his daughter. Victoria was already awake when Isabelle brought her breakfast. Later that day, she slipped into a white dress and looked like a little angel. As she made her way toward the garden, she encountered Thomas in the corridor, who greeted her politely, "Good morning, miss."

"G—good morning," she murmured, avoiding his gaze and making her way to the garden. Upon opening the door, she found Henry watering the flowers. Just as she turned to leave, he stopped her, "Wait, don't go! You need not leave—this is your home."

She hesitated at first, then spoke suddenly. "You work here, is that right?"

"Indeed. I am the gardener. Does that surprise you?"

"A little," she admitted.

"And why, may I ask?"

"Because you're just a boy!"

Henry found her words most displeasing and forced

a laugh. "A boy, you say? I am no boy; I am a man!"

"Certainly not!"

There was a long pause. Henry looked at her with a curious glance. "And how old might you be?"

"I am twelve years old."

"Twelve, you say?"

"Indeed. You seem rather surprised."

"You are quite the peculiar one."

"Me? Peculiar?"

"You're so easily offended, you know."

"You are so rude!"

"And you are spoilt!"

"Hush! I am no such thing!"

"But you are wealthy..." he added. "And wealthy children are oftentimes spoilt."

"Not true!"

"Your name is Victoria, right?"

"Yes—just like Her Majesty, Queen Victoria," she said with an adorable pride.

Henry rolled his eyes. "But you are no queen."

"Are you mocking me?" she replied in an offended tone.

"Oh, not in the least. A name alone does not make one royal. I bear the name of a King, yet I am but a humble gardener."

Victoria fell silent. His boldness and honesty left her quite speechless. He seemed wise beyond his years. "May I ask you a question?" she softened her tone.

"If you will."

"Do you believe in fairy tales?"

"No. And you?"

"Perhaps... but I do believe in God."

"I believe in neither," said the sceptical boy. "My life is punishment enough; why should I believe in foolish tales?"

"What do you mean by that?"

"Never mind. Good day to you, miss."

After saying that, the young gardener turned and walked away quietly. Victoria started to feel guilty. Had she, without meaning to, offended him?

"I wonder what I did. I must have done something," she thought to herself.

CHAPTER 5

TOMORROW IS A NEW DAY

Several days had passed, and Adam had still not returned from London. In his absence, Victoria and Henry had grown rather fond of one another's company, often spending their time together in the garden. An angry voice came through—it was Thomas, calling out for the boy.

"He's calling for you," said Victoria.

"I know," Henry replied.

"And what are you waiting for? He sounds dreadfully angry."

"That is nothing new," he murmured with a heavy sadness.

"He frightens me," Victoria confessed, almost in a whisper. At that moment, Thomas stormed in and was displeased with what he saw. He pointed his finger at him, "Come here at once!"

The boy stepped forward with a stern look, and so

did Thomas. They stood face to face, stared at one another as though they were sworn enemies.

"What is the meaning of this?" Thomas demanded.

"I am working, can't you see?"

"It did not seem so to me. What were you two chattering about?"

"Victoria and I—"

"How dare you address her by name?"

"It is her wish."

"That is unacceptable! You are a servant in this household, boy, and must not forget your place."

Henry rolled his eyes, tired of his constant reproach.

"Do not try my patience," said Thomas.

"Leave me be!"

"Mind yourself, you insolent boy! I shall not warn you again."

"And if I wish to spend time with her?" the boy asked without a hint of fear. "What then? What will you do?"

Thomas paused for a moment. "You shall regret it."

He forbade Henry from maintaining any sort of friendship with Victoria. But why? What could he possibly gain by keeping them apart? His reasoning remained a mystery—strange and deeply unsettling. Only he knew the truth behind his actions. Henry lowered his head, eyes red with fury. He bit his lip, clenched his fists, and tried to contain the storm of emotions raging inside him. Victoria approached slowly, unaware of what had been said but sensing something was amiss. One look at Henry's face told her all she needed to know.

"He scolded you, didn't he?"

"Do not trouble yourself over it."

"Tell me if he did," she insisted. "because Papa will hear of it. I swear it!"

"Nonsense!" he shouted. "There's no need to tell anyone."

"Then how come you are so upset?"

"Because he..." Henry was about to reveal something, but instead turned away, bearing the secret with him. Victoria's heart sank as she watched him struggle in silence. But she did not dare confront Thomas alone. *"When are you coming home, Papa?"* she thought, longing for the one person who might make sense of it all.

...

Daylight was almost gone. Victoria felt a profound

longing for her father, unable to cope with his absence. She waited on the porch, hoping for his return. Each distant neigh of horses convinced her it was his carriage drawing near. Thomas had been looking for her, and when he found her at last, he approached as silently as a shadow. "May I ask what you are doing here, miss?"

She turned to face him. Despite her resentment, she answered quietly: "I'm waiting for my papa."

"I'm afraid he won't be coming today."

"He will," she frowned. "Papa will come. He promised."

It was their first serious conversation, brief as it was. Thomas appeared strict and unpleasant by nature, yet every man harbours a character of his own and conceals secrets within his heart. Secrets he may be too fearful to disclose. The sun disappeared beyond the horizon, and a gentle summer breeze stirred the air. Victoria and Thomas fell into a silence, both gazing toward the golden sunset. Shortly after, he walked away, and she exhaled a quiet relief. Before night had fully settled, Henry's shadow appeared on the road, hands full of belongings. Victoria waved at him, but he pulled his cap over his eyes and didn't react. She stood frozen—confused by his coldness. *"What's come over him? Why didn't he look at me?"* she wondered. Henry ran to the other side, unable to face her. *"Perhaps the old man is right,"* he thought bitterly. *"Perhaps we can never be friends."* Wistful thoughts troubled the young gardener's mind. He was compelled to forsake a friendship he had cherished.

"Maybe he didn't see me?" Victoria whispered to herself. "No, that can't be! I'm certain he did. Then why did he not talk to me?"

From that moment forth, a heavy sorrow overwhelmed her. Grief, sadness, and frustration... consumed her heart. Her once-fragile world sank deeper into melancholy, and all that had once been beautiful within her became distorted by pain. Light gave way to darkness, and trust turned to bitter doubt. "You're all liars," she whispered bitterly to herself. "Papa promised he would return soon, but he lied. Henry said we were friends, and now he won't speak to me."

She stormed into the house and locked herself in her room. Thomas, having overheard her sobs, grew deeply worried. He knocked gently upon the door, but she gave no reply. She had no wish to speak to anyone; a quiet despair had taken hold of her. A desire to vanish from this dreadful world and never return—a terrifying thought for one so young.

"Leave me alone!" she cried, her voice choked with anguish. Thomas and Ruth were awfully worried and begged her to open the door, but to no avail. No one could persuade her. "Be gone, all of you!"

"What shall we do?" Ruth turned to Thomas. Knowing nothing could be done, he answered: "Leave her be."

And after they withdrew, Victoria began to slowly calm herself.

...

Late at night, Ruth sat in the kitchen with Isabelle, sharing a quiet cup of tea. "Good heavens! My heart aches for that poor dear girl," Ruth said. "If only her father were here."

"Why?" asked Isabelle.

"Because he would have known what to do."

"Fear not. She simply misses him, that's all."

"You may be right. That must be it."

Their conversation was interrupted by Thomas, who entered with a troubled expression—one could notice his concern for Victoria.

"What are you two still doing at this hour?"

"Having tea," they replied.

"And what shall become of little Miss Victoria?" Ruth asked.

"There is nothing to be done."

"The poor girl hasn't eaten a thing..."

"She will not eat, even if we beg," Thomas added before bidding, "Good night."

"Ugh, what an insufferable man!" Isabelle muttered under her breath. Ruth said nothing, finishing her tea in silence. Before going to bed, she passed by Henry's room to tell him good night. There he lay, lost in pensive thought. She sat beside him, brushing her hand through his hair. "What troubles you, my son?"

"It's nothing, Mother," he replied wearily.

"You cannot deceive me."

Henry then looked into his mother's eyes and gave her a tight embrace. "You know me too well."

"I am your mother, after all."

"Why does he hate me so?"

"Oh Henry... please."

"I have done him no wrong."

"Rest now, my son. Tomorrow is a new day."

"It will be the same for me. Another day in prison," he said, voice heavy with pain.

"Do not say such things, Henry, I beg you. Come now, try to sleep. Good night."

"Good night, Mother."

CHAPTER 6

WHISPERS OF THE NIGHT

It was midnight. Victoria heard the faint sound of footsteps approaching her door—then suddenly ceasing. She slipped out of bed, opened the door, and in a trembling voice, called out, "Who's there?" But nobody answered. Looking into the dark corridor, she could see nothing. Though but a child, she was not afraid of the dark. *"How strange!"* she thought. *"I heard footsteps, but no one's there. Could it have been Henry? No—it cannot be! It is late; he must surely be asleep by now."*

After inspecting the corridor, she returned to her bedroom and closed the door behind her. Then, all of a sudden, a white spark flickered, but faded within seconds. "What was that?" she muttered, frightened, leaning against the door. Slowly, she stepped out onto the balcony to investigate. The faint glow had seemed to emerge from the garden below, but it vanished into thin air. "Who's there?" she called again. Nobody answered, only the whispers of the night. Perhaps it was a trick of the moonlight... or something beyond a child's imagination. Who could say?

...

The following day brought nothing extraordinary. Victoria remained upset with her father, who had not written at all. The very morning, she had decided she would not speak to anyone. As she came down the stairs, there was a strange silence in the house. She stepped into the yard: no one was there. Passing through the kitchen, still not a soul. Moving into the dining room, she glanced around the table and saw breakfast laid out, prepared by Ruth. Then, murmured to herself, "There's no one here." As her eyes settled on the food, her stomach growled. It had been nearly two days since she had last eaten. After a while, she sensed someone behind her. It was Thomas who greeted her with a warm "Good morning," as usual. She did not respond and continued eating. Despite her coldness, he spoke again: "You might be wondering where everyone has gone." Victoria finished her meal, rose from the table, and made her way onward, acting as though he did not exist. And he understood her childish and reckless behavior. As she approached the door leading to the garden, she paused and recalled the spark from the previous night. Her eyes drifted beyond the door—a strange sensation that a magic kingdom lay just beyond, waiting to be discovered. Stepping into the garden, all seemed normal. She sat beneath the shade of an old tree and let her thoughts wander. For a moment, it came to her—she was utterly alone. No one to comfort her, no one to speak to. And yet, in that solitude, she found peace. A sense of relief, nourished by the garden's enchanting beauty: the cheerful song of birds, the sweet scent of flowers. She had a hundred reasons not to feel alone in that place. *"This is my paradise. I will stay here forever."*

As she lay upon the green grass, the sun cast its golden light softly across her face. She closed her eyes and began to hum a gentle melody to herself. This was her moment. And in that very moment, each doubt, sorrow, and ache began to fade away. Sweet sleep carried her into the mysterious realm of dreams—a world unknown.

"Victoria! Victoria!"

It was that same familiar voice—the one that always accompanied her dreams. Whose voice was it? Why did it call her? What did it seek? Was it a warning? Her conscience? A memory? The voice followed her everywhere—through dreams and reality.

"I am frightened!" Victoria found herself wandering in a dream of darkness and emptiness. But it was not darkness that terrified her. No, it was something deeper: loneliness. The greatest fear known to man. A dread more powerful than death itself.

"I am frightened! Get me out of here!" she was delirious... as if under a spell. Trapped within a never-ending nightmare. As she spoke in confusion, she suddenly felt a gentle touch upon her shoulder. Her eyes opened, and there he was— her noble and dashing father. Without hesitation, she threw herself into his arms.

"Papa!"

"Have you missed me?" he smiled gracefully.

"Terribly! Don't ever leave me again. Pomise me."

"I promise," he said.

"A promise is a big word—you must think carefully before you make one."

"Oh, my sweet girl, I've missed you so," said Adam, holding her close to his chest. Then the unexpected happened. Something that had not happened in years. A brief smile appeared on her lips as she rested in her father's arms. It lasted only a second. Adam, however, did not see it—the smile he had longed for most.

"Papa... strange things have been happening to me lately."

"What sort of things?"

"I don't know... but I am scared."

At her words, Adam's expression changed. The two of them sat beneath the tree and spoke of all that had occurred during his absence. She confessed of her friendship with Henry, Thomas's strictness, and the strange noises she had heard the night before. Nothing was left unspoken.

"I do not trust Thomas, Papa," she said suddenly. He turned to her in surprise, raising an eyebrow.

"And why, may I ask? Has he said something to you?"

"Not to me... to Henry."

"And what precisely did he say?"

"I believe he—" Victoria stopped her sentence, for

Thomas was approaching. She was wary of him. Her heart and mind grew uneasy in his presence.

After dinner, they went to bed. When Adam tucked her in that night, he asked gently: "What were you trying to tell me about Thomas?"

"I believe he forbids Henry to speak to me."

"Are you certain?"

"We had become such good friends, and he ruined everything."

Adam did not take her words too gravely, but he promised he would sort out the matter.

"I shall speak to him tomorrow, rest assured."

"Thank you, Papa."

"Now, sleep well, my little fairy."

"Good night, Papa."

CHAPTER 7

TRUE FRIENDSHIP

Her father's return brought Victoria a sense of peace and contentment. After countless restless nights, she finally enjoyed a quiet one—no more bad dreams. Adam, however, had not slept well. Rising early on a misty morning, distraught by his daughter's words concerning Thomas. Later that day, determined to clear his doubts, he summoned him to his study.

"You wished to see me, sir?"

"Yes, Thomas. Do come in!" said Adam, removing his eyeglasses and placing them aside. For he was a man often seen with a book or a pen in hand.

"Is everything all right, sir?"

"I do hope so," Adam replied. "But I should like to have a word with you."

"Certainly, sir."

"I hear that Henry and my daughter have become

friends."

"I should hesitate to call it friendship, if I may speak frankly, sir," Thomas replied earnestly. Adam was in disbelief at his direct response. Perhaps Victoria had been right about him all along.

"And pray, how would you define friendship, Thomas?"

"With the utmost respect, sir..." Thomas cleared his throat, choosing his words carefully. "I do not consider it proper that Miss Victoria should keep company with the boy. The circumstances being what they are... he is but a servant and—"

"Now listen here, Thomas!" Adam interrupted him with quiet authority. "I know very well what you mean, and I do not discount your concerns. Nonetheless... they are but two children in search of companionship."

"But sir—"

"If my daughter wants to call Henry a friend, then no one shall speak against it."

"You cannot mean, sir, that you truly approve of such foolishness?" said Thomas, utterly surprised.

"I think it most beneficial that they spend time together. It will do my daughter good."

Thomas was silent. He could not bring himself to endorse such friendship, for his own reasons. Yet he could not argue further. He was bound to obey. With his pride wounded and most displeased, he gave a short bow. "Is that all, sir?"

"It is. You may go."

"With your permission, sir." With that, Thomas withdrew with fury—for never before had Adam spoken to him in such a manner. Upon passing Henry in the corridor, he turned to him full of anger. "Are you pleased now?"

"I don't know what you mean," said the boy.

"Nothing can break your special friendship now!" Thomas added ironically, before storming off. Ruth watched them from a distance, then hurried over to Henry.

"What happened this time, son?" she called. "Oh, what have you done?"

"Mother, please—be calm."

"I cannot be calm. Why was he so angry?"

"Nothing happened. Only that... he forbade me from being friends with Victoria."

"He may have his reasons. You mustn't—"

"Not you, too, Mother?"

Meanwhile, Isabelle interrupted and told him that Edward—his old childhood friend is asking for him. "I must go," the boy said.

"Henry, we were having a serious conversation, young man—"

"Another time, Mother!" he called over his shoulder as he ran off. At the gate, he met Edward. Unbeknownst to him, Victoria stood behind the garden wall, watching them with jealousy. *"He has a friend,"* she thought bitterly. *"He will not want my company any longer."* She turned her face away and wept quietly. The ache of loneliness returned to her. She had always known solitude; not once in her young life had she known true friendship. Though she knew Henry very little, their bond was exceptional—a bond forged in the garden, where it all began. That magical garden had sparked some hope within her. It was no ordinary place; A place of enchantment, no doubt. Still, one could not help but wonder: who—or what—dwelt there?

...

That evening, the skies darkened, and heavy rain began to fall. Thunder rumbled in the distance, and flashes of lightning lit up the clouds. Frightened,

Victoria crawled into her father's embrace.

"Is the lightning the wrath of God, Papa?" she asked softly.

"No, my sweet girl, I assure you—it is not. God does not punish. He forgives."

"Then... should I forgive, too, Papa?"

"Indeed. Blessed are those who forgive." He then noticed a lingering sadness in her eyes. "Have you spoken to Henry?"

She paused a moment, sighed deeply, and replied: "There's no use in talking to him."

"Is something the matter, my dear?"

"He no longer wishes to be my friend."

"Did he say so?"

"No, but I am quite certain of it."

"Then how can you know? Why not—"

"Let us speak no more of that fool, Papa!"

Rising from her seat, she drew a deep breath, her voice quivering with emotion.

"You do not understand! You do not understand!"

Her voice broke as she turned away. Adam took her gently in his arms and said nothing. She could hear the steady rhythm of his heart, calming her down. The two of them remained silent, as the rain fell softly against the windowpanes. Not even the fiercest thunder could part them now.

...

Later that evening, Henry returned home, his clothes soaked by the summer rain. After changing into dry clothes, a knock sounded at the door. "Come in!" To his astonishment, it was Adam. The young gardener was surprised by the unexpected visit.

"I hope I am not intruding," said Adam with a faint smile.

"No... sir... not at all... please, sir, do come in," Henry stammered, suddenly embarrassed.

"Henry, I have come to speak with you—regarding my daughter."

The boy froze, his heart beating fast. He feared Adam had come to warn him to keep his distance from Victoria. Was he in trouble?

"Sir, I—"

But when Adam told him he may continue his friendship with her, he could hardly believe his ears. The joy and relief were beyond words. In that instant, he felt he might throw himself into the man's arms—were it not so improper.

"You do not object, sir?"

"Nonsense. It is my wish that my daughter understands the nature of true friendship. She is quite unhappy."

"Thank you, sir." Henry bowed with gratitude.

"There is one favour I wish to ask of you," Adam added. "Bring back her smile. That is all I ask. Will you do that for me?"

The boy stood silent for a moment, then placed his hand upon his chest. With quiet pride, he answered: "She will smile again. You have my word, Mr. Flynn."

CHAPTER 8

PRINCESS OF FLOWERS

Henry worked in the garden, crestfallen and with a broken heart—it had been days since Victoria had spoken to him. Ruth watched her son from afar, feeling utterly helpless. Isabelle, seeing her so overcome with sorrow, tried to offer comfort.

"Please, do not be so upset."

"Henry is brokenhearted," Ruth replied, pointing toward him.

"One day, your son shall find happiness."

"One day..." she sighed, her voice heavy with sorrow. "That day remains but a dream."

"If Henry hates the garden, why must he look after it?"

"That, I cannot tell you," Ruth replied, wiping away her tears. She then turned back to her chores, and Isabelle followed silently behind.

...

Victoria took a stroll with her father, not far from home, and Henry followed silently behind. When Adam noticed the boy's approach, he quietly stepped aside, allowing him space to speak with his daughter. Upon seeing him, Victoria's expression darkened with anger. She had done everything to avoid him—had barely left her room, fearing she might cross his path. As she turned to leave, Henry gripped her arm. "Victoria, wait!"

"Let go of me!" she shouted.

"Please, listen to me."

"No!"

Then, Henry dropped to his knees—something he had never done before. Desperation filled his voice. "Forgive me, Victoria."

She stood frozen, silenced by the sight. Proud and stubborn as she was, she could not bear to witness his humiliation. Beneath her coldness was a kind and noble heart.

"Forgive me," the boy continued, his voice quivering. "I know I was wrong to neglect you that day, but I had no choice. You have no idea what it is to be me... Thomas makes my life rather difficult."

The young gardener's sincere words touched her

heart. Gently, Victoria placed her hand upon his shoulder. "All right," she said at last. "I forgive you... But only if you promise never to kneel before me again. Up with you now, you foolish boy!"

Henry slowly lifted his head, and their eyes met— his, a deep green; hers, a bright blue—like earth meeting sky. So different, yet incomplete without the other. He rose to his feet, extended his hand to her, and with a gentle smile, said: "Come with me." Not far away, Adam watched from behind a tree. Ever the loving father, he chose not to interfere, smiling quietly as he beheld the tender moment. He withdrew, content—delighted for them both. The two ran through the green field like children tasting freedom for the very first time. Henry led Victoria to a secluded pond, encircled by flowers of every shape and color, each one vibrant with life. She stood in awe, enchanted by their radiant beauty. Flowers had always brought her joy, evoking the sweetest memories of childhood. Amidst their blooms, she felt as though she belonged. The sun shone brighter that day, casting golden light across the still water. The trees and their leaves whispered old tales and untold secrets.

"How lovely they are."

"I knew you'd love it here," Henry replied.

"The flowers look like…"

"Like a rainbow, do they not?"

"Precisely!"

Henry began picking a few blossoms, selecting each with great care and weaving them into a delicate crown, as only a true gardener might.

"What are you doing?" she asked.

"A gift—for you."

"For me?"

"A crown for Queen Victoria," he said with a teasing smile, then gently placed it upon her head. It was the first time Victoria had ever felt truly seen. Aside from Adam, no one had given her anything so thoughtful. Yet this was more than a gift—it was a gesture made with care, a token of friendship crafted from a genuine heart.

He looked at her and smiled. "Long live the Princess of Flowers!"

"But I am not…"

"You do love flowers, don't you?"

She fell silent. Gratitude rose in her chest, though shyness held back her words. Then, she summoned

her courage, and her voice softened as she spoke.
"Henry..."
"Yes?"
"Thank y..."
"What was that?"
"Thank you—truly. You are very kind."
He offered a warm, friendly smile. "Think nothing
of it. You deserve it."
Victoria lightly touched the flower crown upon her
head, her eyes filled with tears—but this time, they
were tears of joy. Henry observed her with curiosity,
not to see whether she liked his gift, but because he
longed—more than anything—to see her smile. And
then, at last, she did. Little Victoria gave a sweet and
delicate smile. It bloomed like a spring flower after
a long and cold winter, and its brightness seemed to
light the fields around them. She looked so
cheerful—it felt almost like a dream.
Hand in hand, they wandered along the edge of the
pond, their laughter echoing through the trees.
They were full of joy and hope, for it was Henry, the
flowers, and nature itself—who had restored her
innocent smile. Holding her hand a little tighter, the
young gardener looked at the flowers around them

and whispered with quiet gratitude: "Thank you, flowers."

CHAPTER 9

THE GREEN FAIRY — PART I

On a quiet evening filled with memories, Adam sat alone in his armchair, the script titled *'The Green Fairy'* resting gently on his lap. He read it with a deep sense of longing, for within its pages lay the thread that tied him to his fate. His thoughts drifted back to his younger years — a world long gone, now no more than a shadow in his memory.

...

London, 17 December 1840

Snow fell lightly, without a sound. A crowd had gathered before a modest theatre, but dearly loved by the people of London. On a cold December evening, they had come to see the premiere of the much-whispered drama, *The Green Fairy*. Behind the curtain, actors and dancers with scripts in their hands, pacing back and forth, filled with excitement. Among them was the playwright — a twenty-year-old named Adam Flynn, who had begun writing plays at fifteen. *The Green Fairy* marked his first work to reach the public stage. In time, it would become one of his most celebrated works. But for now, he stood alone in a dark corner, overcome with nerves and emotions. It was the first time his play would be performed to an enormous crowd. He feared their judgment—the eyes of the public, the pens of the critics. Word had spread of a young unknown playwright of Irish descent. This had roused curiosity and drawn attention. Five minutes before the curtain would rise, Adam looked around, growing uneasy—someone was missing. The lead actress—the one meant to play the Green Fairy—was nowhere to be seen.

"Paul, where is Avelina?" he asked in a low, urgent voice.

"I don't know. She must be around somewhere." Paul replied with a shrug.

"But... the play is about to begin,"

"I'm here!" called a sweet voice from behind. And there she was—Avelina, lovely as ever. She was just eighteen, fair-haired, vivid green eyes, and a smile so enchanting that it could melt even the coldest heart. She wore a flowing green robe with delicate petals, shimmering wings at her back, and a crown of lilies. Young Adam looked at her with deep affection and tenderness. To him, she looked like a fairy princess stepped out of a dream. His eyes lingered, soft and bright, for he had fallen hopelessly and madly in love—from the very moment he first saw her. Avelina lived with her grandmother, an elderly woman who had taken her in from the orphanage and raised her as her own. Adam first saw her at the theatre—drawn not only by her beauty, but by her manner, and the way her voice breathed life into every word. From that moment, he dreamed of having her act in one of his plays. He was now certain of his feelings for her—but uncertain of hers. Avelina had shown great dedication during rehearsals and mastered her part with a quiet brilliance. She had never once failed him. He was overwhelmed by the play—but far more by the sight of her.

"I am pleased to see you, Avelina. May I ask where you have been?"

"I apologize," she replied in a low voice. "My grandmother is gravely ill, and I could not leave her unattended..."

"I'm very sorry to hear it," his voice softened. "You must not trouble yourself."

From behind the curtain came a voice: "Two minutes, ladies and gentlemen!"

"I wish you good luck," he said with a warm smile. She turned to him, her eyes glowing with gratitude. She offered her thanks before walking away light as a fairy.

...

The play had ended. A thunder of applause filled the air. "*Magnificent!!... Brilliant!!... Exquisite performance!... Bravo!!*" Cheers and praise filled the theater. Avelina truly shone as the Green Fairy, receiving many flattering comments from those present. She curtsied with grace, feeling humbled and honoured by the adoration. Compliments were given to Adam as well, who was over the moon. Later, when the theatre lay in quiet solitude, he felt the time had come to declare his love to her. With only the two of them remaining, he took a deep breath and stepped forward. But just as he opened his mouth to speak, suddenly, a voice echoed through the hall: "Avelina, Avelina, your grandmother, she—"

The young lady was filled with dread. "What is it? What has happened to my grandmother?"

"I have only just received word... My deepest condolences."

In that instant, she sank to her knees; her heart broke into pieces. She had just received the cruelest news—that she had lost the one person who had loved her truly. Once more, she was alone. How unfortunate!

"No, no..." her voice breaking as she wept. "My grandmother... This cannot be... It cannot be true..."

Adam felt a deep sorrow; he longed to go to her, to offer comfort, but feared his presence might be unwelcome in her moment of anguish. So he stood silently aside, watching as others gathered around her. Yet no words of comfort could reach her broken heart. Then, without a word, she rose and fled into the night, leaving faint footprints on the white snow. Adam watched her leave, her sorrow becoming his own. Meanwhile, he heard harsh laughter and bitter words. *"Poor creature... Now she'll be all alone,"... "I have no pity. People say she was never fond of her grandmother,"... "No, no—it was the grandmother who could not stand her,"... "Who would care for an orphan, especially one without a penny to her name?"* Spoken by the very people who had claimed to be her friends. Their hearts, it seemed, were as cold as the snow. Adam turned sharply, his face pale with disbelief. *"How could they speak of Avelina with such cruelty?"* he thought. Their words were empty lies—nothing but idle gossip. He could no longer stay silent. "Enough! Speak no ill of her! Have you no shame? You know nothing of her life." Suddenly, all fell silent, they were ashamed.

...

After the death of her grandmother, Avelina never returned to the theatre. Upon hearing the news, Adam was deeply saddened—but he understood. Once, he sent her a note, asking to meet. But she never came. As Christmas drew near, his longing to see her only grew stronger. He had to find her—no matter the cost.

A friend from the theatre, Catherine, had delivered the letter and knew of Avelina's whereabouts. But she would not reveal it. Still, Adam would not give up so easily. "Catherine, please," he pleaded. "Tell me where she is."

"I cannot," she answered. "I promised her I wouldn't tell a soul."

"I must see her. That is all I ask."

"She does not wish to see anyone."

"Then tell her to meet me, just once. I give you my word—I will not trouble her again."

Catherine hesitated, then looked into his desperate eyes. She saw something in them that moved her—something honest and pure. After a pause, she told him when and where he might find Avelina.

"If you truly love her, she deserves to know," Catherine said, before walking away with a smile upon her lips.

CHAPTER 10

THE GREEN FAIRY — PART II

London, 23 December 1840

The city was wrapped in the warm spirit of Christmas. The festive season filled every corner, while a blanket of white snow covered the pavements. Near a glowing fire, carolers sang sweet Christmas carols while children laughed, sliding and playing in the snow. Catherine had told Adam where to find Avelina, and now he waited there, restless and anxious. The air was bitterly cold, and the dim glow of lamps cast long shadows on the silent streets. At last — footsteps on the snow. He turned — and his heart nearly stopped. There she was. He had to restrain himself from crying out. And this, he knew, would be his last chance to speak with her. Avelina stood alone, a small suitcase in her hand, waiting for someone. Adam approached her quietly, like a shadow. Suddenly, she turned to face him, her eyes wide with surprise and confusion. She had not expected him to be there.

"How are you, Avelina? How lovely to see you."

The dim lights revealed the sorrow written across his face. She did not answer him. Instead, she turned away, looking anywhere but at him. Despite her coldness, he could not remain silent.

"I have come to offer you my—"

"What do you want of me?" she spoke at last.

"Please accept my sincere condolences on the passing of your grandmother," said the dashing young Adam.

"Thank you kindly," she replied with courtesy. "Is that why you came?"

"Not entirely. I must speak with you."

Avelina's green eyes looked at him with a sorrow beyond words. She was terribly alone.

"You wouldn't know," she said, her voice heavy with pain. "You wouldn't know what it is to have no one—no one but yourself."

"You insult me. I know that all too well."

"I don't believe you. You have a family."

"I have not."

She noted an unusual side of Adam. No longer did

he appear to be the charming young playwright so often admired by society. Before her now stood the true Adam: vulnerable, and profoundly alone.

"My mother and father have long since passed," he murmured. "And my brother... he fled from me as far as he was able."

There was a silence around them. In the distance, faint voices echoed—those of men, women, and children. The snow, which had briefly paused, began to fall again. They looked at each other with sorrowful eyes, yet no words were exchanged. Something deep within forbade her to turn him away. For she loved him too, though only in secret. It was a love she thought impossible: he, a gentleman of means; she, a humble orphan. After a long pause, she exhaled heavily and opened her heart to him.

"Do you recall the night of the play?"

Adam nodded and paid attention.

"My grandmother had fallen very ill, and I was unwilling to go to the play, but she begged: '*Go, dearest. It is my wish that you shine tonight.*'... I was scared to leave her, yet she insisted. '*You shall find me here, waiting for you.*' Those were her final words." Avelina's voice broke as she continued. "It is all my fault! Had I stayed by her side, perhaps she might—"

"You mustn't blame yourself!" said Adam, stepping forward. "How could you have known? I assure you that your grandmother wished to spare you the sorrow—"

"Forgive me," she interrupted. "But I must go."

Meanwhile, the sound of hooves upon fresh snow grew louder. A carriage approached and stopped beside her. It was time for Avelina to leave—perhaps never to return. Adam was unable to accept the cruel reality unfolding before him. He was losing her—she would soon be gone forever.

"Wait, don't go!" he cried. "You do not wish to leave—I see it in your eyes."

"I am most grateful for your kindness... but I must go now."

He stepped closer, his heart pounding. "There is something I must tell you,"

"Farewell, Mr. Flynn," she murmured, stepping toward the carriage door. But Adam stopped her, proclaiming aloud: "I love you, Avelina!"

She paused in the midst of the stillness, her suitcase

slipped from her trembling hands and landed softly upon the snow. Adam stepped forward, "You have my heart, Avelina. I cannot bear to lose you."

She stood at a crossroads—torn between two destinies. One path led to her distant cousin, promising a life of stability and certainty; the other to Adam—a man who had just declared a love most sincere.

"We must leave, miss! We haven't much time!" called the coachman.

From the other side, Adam pleaded once more, "Stay with me. I swear I'll make you happy."

Then, without turning her head, she stepped into the carriage and whispered *Farewell* through tears.

Just like that, Adam watched the woman he loved slip away, vanish into the shadows of the night. His heart sank. He walked down the long, desolate road, for nothing, at that moment, was colder than his own heart. Yet what happened moments later would remain with him all the days of his life.

"Adam!!" called a voice from behind. It was Avelina, hurrying toward him through the falling snow. Without a word, they fell into each other's arms. "What made you come back?" he asked, full of joy.

"Because I love you," she confessed with emotion. "Oh, I always have. I was simply too afraid to say it." To Adam, her words were as sacred as a hymn — the sweetest melody ever sung by angels. He had longed for that confession in silence. They had loved one another secretly — until this moment.

"Will you marry me?" he asked so unexpectedly.

"Yes — oh, yes!" she exclaimed with laughter in her eyes. "My heart is yours — now and always."

...

They were wed within a year. Adam and Avelina were deeply and blissfully in love. Their union was soon blessed with the birth of a daughter, Victoria — whom they adored above all else, regarding her as their most precious gift. Yet when Victoria was but six years old, Avelina passed away. Her death was as mysterious as it was devastating; she was found lifeless in the garden of their home. Years passed, and her sudden loss weighed heavily upon both father and daughter, bringing them profound grief and despair.

Adam's love story had begun so beautifully, only to end in tragedy — much like the plays he so often wrote. Yet such is the nature of life: as cruel as it may seem, death clings more to us than even our own shadow.

CHAPTER 11

ILLUSION OR ENCHANTMENT

Victoria and Henry had become quite inseparable—true friends in every sense. For the first time in many years, she smiled again, and Adam could not fathom how Henry had achieved what he had long failed to accomplish. *"I gave her everything,"* he thought. *"And yet, none of it brought her joy."* After all that had happened, his regard for the young gardener only deepened. The boy had kept his promise, and for that alone, Adam was more than willing to grant him whatever his heart might desire. Yet the boy's request seemed rather odd, perhaps a bit silly. Henry's wish was to protect Victoria for all the days of his life. A peculiar wish, indeed—is it not?

...

September arrived quietly, bringing cooler mornings, though the afternoons remained mild and pleasant. Adam had invited a small circle of friends—literary gentlemen with whom he maintained a close fellowship. Thomas was attending to the guests, while Ruth and Isabelle busied themselves in the kitchen. Meanwhile, Victoria and Henry had gone for a stroll, enjoying very fine weather. The countryside was unlike London in every possible way, and she was quite enchanted by its beauty.

"Henry, why don't you believe in God?" she took a bite from an apple as they walked along.

Henry looked at her, surprised. "Why do you ask me that?"

"You once said your life feels like a prison. Is that why you've lost faith?"

"Oh, Victoria," he sighed heavily. "Pay it no mind."

There was much she longed to know about him—but Henry remained unwilling to share the matters of his heart. After wandering around for two hours, they returned home. Unaware of the guests, they noticed two unfamiliar horse-drawn carriages and wondered who might have come to visit. "Who could it be?" Victoria asked and Henry shrugged. From within the guest room came unfamiliar

voices—gentlemen engaged in lively conversation.
The two young rascals crouched quietly behind the
door. *"Who are these men?... Do you know them?... I've
not seen them before,"* they began whispering among
themselves. But unbeknownst to them, Thomas
stood behind—arms crossed, and a stern look on his
face. "What are you two doing there?" Their hearts
nearly stopped, as though they had seen a ghost. So
they mumbled an excuse that they were only
passing through. Thomas said nothing more, but
with a slight nod, he made it clear that they leave at
once. They ran off, like two frightened children
caught red-handed.

...

The guests stayed until late, then departed one by
one. The calm September night brought a warm
breeze; the leaves had yet to fall, and the garden
looked lovelier than ever. Victoria knocked softly on
her father's door. Upon entering, she found him fast
asleep. "Oh, he's asleep," she whispered. A script
was resting in his hands. Gently, she took it from
him and read the title: *'The Green Fairy by Adam
Flynn.'* Sitting on the edge of the bed, she carefully
flipped through the pages, reading in silence. Soon

after, sleep overcame her. She closed her eyes and curled up near her father's feet. And she dreamed — as always. But this dream was unlike any other. In the vast emptiness, a voice echoed from afar. The same voice she had heard before. It called her name once more. She saw nothing — only darkness. "*Victoria…*" the voice echoed again, louder this time. "*Who are you? Answer me!*" she demanded. The sound grew louder, so she couldn't even hear her own thoughts. "*Who's calling me? Do I know you? Show yourself!*" Victoria shouted into the void of her dream. Absolute silence. The peculiar voice never stayed long enough to answer. Night after night, it would return to haunt her in her sleep. She had grown rather tired of it. A voice that had become an endless nightmare: a nameless whisper in the dark. And then, out of nowhere, a sudden and blinding light pierced through — chasing away the shadows. Before her stood a strange, glimmering figure. Though she carried the likeness of a woman, she was no human — She was a fairy. Her ears were long and pointed — markings of an ancient and ethereal lineage. Thin golden eyes and hair, white as snow, reaching to her feet. Skin, pale as moonlight and nearly translucent—Pure enchantment. She was a celestial beauty, a flower that thrives forevermore. Her flowing white robe shimmered beneath the starlight. This was no creature of flesh and blood; she belonged to a realm beyond the living—no mere mortal could ever possess such grace. Then, with a faint yet luminous smile, she faded away into the darkness, like an illusion or enchantment.

Victoria opened her eyes, aware she had been dreaming. And yet, it was more than a mere dream. Who was that strange, unearthly figure—so unlike anything of this world? Why had she not said a single word? Could there be some bond linking her to the voice that called from the shadows? Had it been but a figment of her imagination, sparked by her father's manuscript? Or an idle dream? Well... only a dream. And yet, perhaps that peculiar vision was bound with Victoria's real world.

That mysterious, magical being who had at last revealed herself might hold the key to unlock the door of secrets. Secrets and charms waiting to be unraveled. A beginning, or perhaps an end. Or... the start of a never-ending nightmare.

CHAPTER 12

LITTLE DREAMER

"Papa, Papa!" A voice, both frightened and thrilled, echoed through the room. The morning sunlight had already slipped through the curtains. Victoria had awakened from her vivid dream—one that had stirred her heart as much as her mind. She could hardly wait to tell Adam everything, detail by detail. "Papa, Papa... wake up!"

Adam opened his weary eyes and found her pale, anxious face leaning over him. "What is it, in Heaven's name?" he asked, rubbing his eyes. "Why do you shout so early?"

"I've something important to tell you!"

"What has happened?"

"Papa... you won't believe it! I had the most unusual dream, and—"

But Adam did not let her finish: "A dream? You wake me for such foolishness?"

"But Papa," she pleaded, "this one was different. It felt... real."

"Unbelievable," he muttered.

"Papa, I—"

"I shall hear no more of that!" he shouted, quickly rising from his bed. Victoria fell into silence; never before had he addressed her in such a harsh tone. "I've had enough of your silly dreams!" he continued. "Always the same tale: I dreamed this... I dreamed that..."

"But Papa—"

"No more fairy stories, Victoria!" he said firmly. "You must put aside foolish fancies and childhood whims. It is time to grow up."

Those harsh words struck like lightning, shattering Victoria's fragile heart. The air between them grew heavy with tension. Their eyes met, and neither spoke. A dreadful silence filled the room, broken only by the soft chirping of birds outside the window. For an instant, Adam felt a terrible remorse. Yet it was far too late. He saw the pain in her wide, wounded blue eyes. A simple apology would not mend what was already broken. Bruised by her father's words, she clenched her small hands and bit her lip to hold back the tears. Adam said nothing, no words of solace falling from his lips — none that could reach her now. "You do not understand," she murmured in a whimpering voice. "I... I only wished you would believe me..." Then, closing her eyes briefly, she turned to him with the most destructive words: "I hate you, Papa!" Before he could find a word to say, she stormed out in fury. Adam felt a sharp ache in his chest — Those words cut through him like a dagger. "What have I done?" he murmured, burying his face in his hands. It felt like a bad dream. The warmth of that peaceful September morning had unraveled into something unbearable. And he knew, without a doubt, that he alone was to blame — none other but himself.

...

Later that day, he sat at the table, alone, his heart heavy with regret. He could not bring himself to eat. His gaze remained fixed upon Victoria's empty chair. Only Thomas, the faithful old servant, remained at his side.

"Your soup's gone cold, sir."

Adam gave a faint, pitiful look. "Why do I fail to comprehend her? I find myself utterly unable to fathom the nature of her world."

"She is only a child. You must have patience, sir."

Adam shook his head slowly. "No... she is unlike any other. Why is it that we cause our children pain, Thomas?"

Thomas listened with earnest attention, and he could see the sorrow written all over his face.

"May I ask... Is something the matter? You seem deeply upset this morning."

"I have not felt thus since I lost my wife, and now..." Adam sighed painfully. "Victoria told me she hates me."

"Surely, she did not truly mean it."

"You don't know my daughter well."

Thomas recalled Victoria's somber demeanor during Adam's absence. "Do not despair, sir."

"She is all I have."

"Rest assured, all shall be well," Thomas said, trying to offer comfort. Just beyond the doorway, Isabelle had been eavesdropping. She hurried to share the news. "Ruth, Ruth... you won't believe what I've just overheard!"

Ruth raised a brow. "And what might that be, this time?"

"Mr. Flynn and his little girl appeared to have argued this very morning!"

"And where did you hear such nonsense?"

"I heard him telling Thomas."

Ruth gave her a reproachful look, then tapped lightly on her head with a wooden spoon. "You ought to be ashamed of yourself, impudent girl!"

"Oh my dear head!" Isabelle exclaimed. "Why did you do that?"

"So you might learn not to stick your nose where it doesn't belong."

Just then, Henry entered, immediately sensing the tension. "What's going on here?"

"Oh, Henry! Your mother has gone mad—she hit me with a spoon!"

"Hear, hear!" he chuckled. "Well, I do wonder why..."

"Do not mock me," Isabelle pouted.

"That's quite enough!" Ruth said sharply. "Stop behaving like a child and be gone at once!"

...

Little Victoria sat alone in her room, sobbing quietly. Lost in fragile thoughts, she remained wrapped in the gentle innocence of childhood.

Each time she closed her eyes, her father's voice echoed through her mind: *"No more fairy stories, Victoria! It is time to grow up."* She wiped away her tears and whispered to herself, *"I simply won't do it! My dreams are trying to tell me something... and I must find out what it is."*

What could she have meant by that? Dreams revealing truths?... *A little dreamer*, that's what she was. And though children must grow, dreams remain unchanged, the same as the moon. No one would believe her, of course. But that would not stop her from dreaming until she unraveled their secrets.

Yet... do dreams truly harbour secrets?

CHAPTER 13

NO MORE FAIRY TALES!

The full silver moon hung high in the black sky, encircled by a thousand stars. The night was silent—haunting, and strangely magical. Nothing could be heard but the wind, whistling and whispering through leaves. The world was asleep. All, but Victoria. She sat in her chair like a ghost among shadows, drifting in a sea of restless thoughts—A wanderer beneath the stars. She was waiting, hoping the mysterious being would appear once more. She had questions—so many questions. Sometimes even wondered: *"Could it be? Mama... have you come back to me?"*

Her eyes, swollen and red from hours of crying, stared into the deep darkness. And yet she was awake—more fully than she had ever been. Beneath the full moon, Victoria whispered into the night: *"Where is she? Why isn't she coming?"*

For nearly two hours, she had sat in restless silence. Just as sleep began to creep over her, the balcony door creaked open—on its own. A fierce wind stormed into the room, howling like a wild spirit. Startled from her brief rest, she fell from the chair, her heart pounding, and hurried to shut the door. Mesmerized by the moon's ethereal beauty, she was unaware of the wonder unfolding below. In the moonlit garden, the flowers danced gracefully with luminous colours.

"What are those?" she whispered. "Fireflies?"

She leaned over the balcony, drawn by a spark or a distant sound, but could not see clearly. She needed to know—to assure herself it wasn't another dream. After that, she went down the stairs with careful and light steps. Passed through the darkened corridor, as a silver thread of moonlight streamed through the windows following her like a quiet companion. At last, she reached the garden door—but to her great disappointment, it was locked. "What a pity!" she sighed softly. "What ought I do now?"

Victoria pressed her ear gently against the door, attempting to hear any sound from the garden beyond. Something strange—something magical—

was unfolding out there. Her deep longing to see it for herself was so strong that the door opened slowly, as though the demands of her heart had cast a spell. As she stepped forward, it took longer than expected for her eyes to adjust—and when they did, there was nothing. "No," she breathed. "That can't be. Where did the fireflies go?"

All the joy and excitement turned into a great disappointment. Had it all been her imagination?

"Papa is right," she said to herself. *"No more fairy tales, Victoria!"*

Disheartened and crestfallen, she turned away. But before she could take a second step, a voice—soft, familiar, and filled with quiet power—called to her: "Turn around, Victoria!"

Guided by the sound, she slowly turned back toward the garden... And what she saw stole her breath away.

...

The following morning, Adam rose with the dawn, having spent a restless night. Like a desperate father, he wandered to his daughter's door but lacked the courage to knock, fearful of rejection. He was a man with a soft heart, particularly in matters concerning

his girl. Convinced she was still asleep, he quietly
withdrew and made his way to the kitchen.

"Ruth, would you be so kind as to prepare Victoria's
breakfast?"

"Right away! And yourself, Mr. Flynn?"

"I have no appetite, but thank you," he replied, then
left without another word.

"Poor thing!" exclaimed Isabelle. "Whatever
happened to him? He looked quite miserable." With
a mischievous smile, she then added: "Yet, he is
rather handsome... is he not, Ruth?"

"Put a stop to that nonsense, will you?"

"Imagine if he married me. Ah!" Isabelle sighed
dreamily. Ruth rolled her eyes in disbelief.

What had happened the night before? What had
Victoria seen when she turned her head? Some time
later, Ruth knocked several times upon her door but
received no answer. "Miss, please open the door,"
she called gently. Then, growing worried, she
hurried to Adam's study, where he stood
thoughtfully by the window.

"I am sorry to trouble you, sir, but..."

"Yes, Ruth?"

"Miss Victoria isn't responding. Would you mind

seeing if she's well?"

Adam rushed to her room at once. Finding the door locked, he requested the spare key. Upon opening it, he was relieved to see Victoria sleeping peacefully in her bed. His eyes glanced across the room, and the floor was covered with flowers, petals, and leaves.

"What is the meaning of this?" he asked, turning to Ruth.

"I could not say, sir," she replied with a shrug.

The petals were scattered on the floor and even on her bed, where she lay like an angel on a cloud. Both Adam and Ruth were astonished and silent. Neither could fathom what had taken place.

"Oh, look! The balcony door is open!" Ruth observed.

Adam stepped forward and closed the door, sweeping petals aside with his foot. He then looked out over the garden below. "Could the wind have carried them in?"

"It must've been quite windy last night to cause all this mess," Ruth said, before excusing herself. A short while later, Henry entered, cap in hand. "Mother said you wished to see me, sir?"

"Yes, Henry! Do come in—and behold this."

The boy stepped in and saw Victoria's room overtaken by garden flowers.

"Oh... how wonderful!" he whispered. Adam gave him a strange look, raising an eyebrow.

"Oh—pardon me, sir, I just—"

"Would you be good as to explain all that?"

"They appear to be from my garden, sir—indeed they do," Henry replied quickly.

"I am well aware of that. But how pray, did they find their way into this room?"

"I haven't the slightest idea, sir. Perhaps it was the wind? You ought to ask Victoria."

"I doubt she'd tell me anything."

"May I ask why, sir?"

Adam hesitated. "Yesterday... she told me..."

All of a sudden, Victoria awoke to find her bed covered in flowers. Henry greeted her with a cheerful "Good morning," while Adam remained silent. Without a word, she rose and went directly to Henry, embracing him for the first time, disregarding her father's presence. Who turned away and quietly left the room.

"Is something the matter, Victoria?" Henry asked,

surprised by her sudden behavior.

"Oh, Henry, do you see this? Isn't my room lovely?" she exclaimed, ignoring his concern.

"Indeed, it is," he agreed with a smile. "But how did all these flowers get here?"

"Does it matter?" she said while gathering a handful of petals and throwing them into the air. Then she began to twirl and hum to herself. He observed her in silence. Her behavior was unnatural, as if some strange charm had overtaken her spirit. That day, she was not quite herself. Henry asked again: "What is the matter with you?"

"I don't know what you mean."

"You are not yourself," he replied. "You frighten me."

"This is who I am," she claimed with absolute certainty.

"Now tell me, why would you not speak to your poor father?"

She stopped at once, her mood shifted, and her voice grew cold. "I shall never speak to him again."

"Surely you don't mean that? He is your father."

"He is a bad father."

The boy was shaken by the cruelty of her words.

"That is absurd! You are being childish... and unjust."

"How dare you?" she shouted. "You know nothing, you fool!"

"Perhaps I am a fool," he said, "but there is one thing I know, that you—"

"That I what?"

"That you are heartless... and ungrateful!" his words escaping before he could stop them.

"Why do you say that to me?"

"Because it is the truth," he continued, his voice unsteady as he turned away to hide his tears. "Your father adores you—and you cannot even see it. I would give anything to have a father like him."

Victoria had caused him pain—yet she was only a child, impulsive and careless with her words. Truly, she did not mean it, when she said: "You should count yourself fortunate to have no father at all."

Henry was in disbelief; he no longer recognized her. Her words, her demeanor, and her sudden unkindness—they were all foreign. Who was this girl before him?

"I wish you hadn't said that," he whispered, and left brokenhearted. Victoria simply stood there, silent amidst the sea of flowers. It seemed to her that the whole world had turned against her. All had forsaken her—all but the flowers, for they alone remained faithful.

CHAPTER 14

JAMES GREEN

After having argued with Victoria, Henry went out into the garden, seeking occupation and peace for his mind.

"What is the matter with you, boy?" Thomas asked as he approached.

But Henry gave no reply. He did not even turn his head; he had no intention of answering. Of all things he loathed most, was to reveal his weakness before others. Thomas stepped closer. "Speak! What has happened?"

"Why do you ask? As though you truly care..." Henry exhaled sharply. "My misery rather pleases you."

Thomas shook his head and with an ironic smirk, said: "I warned you, but you would not listen."

"You know nothing!"

"I have told you—there can never be a friendship

between you and her. There will be an obstacle far too great."

"What obstacle?"

"You are so gullible... same as—" he hesitated.

"As whom? Say it! Finish your sentence!" Henry demanded, staring at him with fierce eyes. Thomas, however, dared not meet his eyes. For within those green eyes lay a painful reminder of a sorrowful past. The boy reminded him too much of someone he had loved so dearly—his only son, *James.*

...

Fifteen years ago, that house and its garden were far from ordinary. Mysteries and untold stories dwelt in every corner and room. Secrets that were never spoken in that home. It had belonged to David Flynn, Adam's grandfather, and his faithful right-hand was Walter Green, Thomas's father. Upon David's passing, the estate fell under the supervision of the Green family. Since Adam's father made no use of it, it was proclaimed that one of his sons should eventually inherit the property. Thomas had a son named James, who was twenty-four years old. His wife had left him when their son was four, without so much of a reason or farewell.

At that time, he lived in the house alongside his son and a young woman named Ruth. She was the daughter of one of his cousins. James was a gardener and adored his work. This infuriated Thomas, who urged him to abandon the garden and build a life elsewhere. But the gardener remained loyal to his passion. For his heart belonged to the flowers and the earth.

"James! Are you still here?" called Thomas.

"Yes, father!" he replied, as he continued to dig, his hands and garments covered in mud.

"Look at you, son!"

"Please, leave me be, Father!"

He often preferred the company of himself. And his stubbornness displeased his father greatly, as he often tried to keep his son's life in order. Perhaps it was selfishness, yet he did so out of a profound love for him. And who could have imagined that someone as Thomas was capable of love? Life is full of surprises, especially the human heart—an ocean deep with secrets.

"Time to leave this accursed garden!"

"It is not accursed. Father, please..."

At times, James found it quite difficult to get along

with him. Though he deeply respected him, he could not endure his constant meddling in his affairs. Angered by his son's obstinacy, Thomas left in frustration. Meanwhile, Ruth came and offered him a glass of water. "Have a drink."

"You are most kind, Ruth."

Even in her younger years, Ruth had never been much of a talker; more inclined to listen than to offer advice. She was a spirited young lady who boldly declared she would never marry, for she would be no man's wife. In a time when unmarried women faced harsh judgment, she remained true to herself. She and James got along remarkably well, bound by a quiet, mutual understanding.

"This garden is lovely."

"To my father, it's an abomination," he replied with a weary sigh.

"Why ever would he think so?"

"He can't accept the fact that I'm a gardener—and nothing more."

"I see nothing wrong with that. You do honest work."

"He would have me be something I am not," James said, turning his attention back to the roses. He worked in the garden by day and often spent the nights there. This habit of his angered his father all the more.

One warm summer night, James lay asleep in his garden beneath the sky full of stars. Suddenly, he was awakened by whispers softly calling his name. *"James… James… James!"*

"Ruth? Is that you?" he called, his voice echoing through the stillness of the night. All of a sudden, a radiant light broke through the darkness. Then came the voices—strange and unfamiliar—calling his name again.

"Who are you?" he demanded.

"We are the flowers of the garden, James!" the voices answered all at once.

"Well, bless my soul!" he murmured, stepping back. "Are you… Are you real?"

The voices spoke once more, louder than before: "James! If you wish for your garden to flourish for all eternity… then you must do something for us—something only you can fulfill."

None of it made any sense to him. He could no longer tell whether he was dreaming or descending into madness.

"For you alone hold the power to save us!"

"To save you?"

"Only you can prevent our extinction," the voices continued. "Should you fail to give your life for our flowers, we shall cease to exist, and with our demise, your garden shall perish as well."

"What do you mean?" James cried, trembling and confused. "Why do you speak in riddles? Who are you? Reveal yourselves!"

Then, from the shadows, a single, delicate voice spoke: "We are the fairies of this garden." And a figure stepped into the pale light. A white fairy the size of a human. James gazed upon her, enchanted by her ethereal beauty. "What do you want from me?" he asked earnestly.

"Only one thing," the white fairy replied.

"And what might that be?"

"Your precious life."

"My life?" James gasped, in disbelief at what he heard. "Why would you want my life?"

"Your life is the key to our salvation."

"You mean to say... that you would have me die for your sake?"

"James, if we perish... your garden shall perish with

us. Is that what you truly want?"

He understood, at last, that it was the fairies who breathed life into his cherished garden. The thought that his sacrifice might work a miracle filled him with profound joy. For the first time in all his years, he felt a purpose. He had ever lived solely for that garden, treating it as a sacred temple. The fairies persuaded him with ease—his faith in nature easily deceived him. Was he, perhaps, under a spell? He felt no fear for his life.

"What must I do?" James said, after a long silence.

"Simply close your eyes and we shall do the rest."

His mind turned to his poor father. He knew his absence would break Thomas's heart. It would bring him unbearable sorrow and despair.

"But my father? How can I leave him?"

The white fairy drew forth a golden pendant, inscribed with the words: *"I AM ALWAYS HERE."*

"What may this be?"

"It is for your father."

"To what purpose? He will not understand."

"He is well aware of our existence."

"What? How can that be?"

"We have revealed ourselves to him and told him

that you are the chosen one."

"And how did he react?"

"He called us an abomination and vowed never to allow such a thing."

"So, when he finds this pendant, he will know that my time has come. That will surely break his heart," he sighed, knowing nothing could be done.

"That is not all," said the white fairy. "He who gives his life for us shall leave a mark."

"What do you mean by that?"

"You shall be reborn — by another woman's womb."

"Goodness!" cried James. "How can such a thing be possible?"

"With our magic, all things are possible. When you become one with the garden, a part of you shall remain here, and the rest shall be reborn in a boy."

"Might he resemble me?"

"He shall wear your face... but not your soul."

"And the woman who —?"

"None other than Ruth. She shall carry the child made by our magic."

James had a thousand questions racing through his mind; each answer only deepened his doubts. "My father... will not lose me forever," he whispered.

"There is something you must know," the white fairy added. "The child shall never be free."

"What do you mean?"

"He is to serve the fairy garden, ever bound as its faithful guardian."

James frowned. "I do not understand. A prisoner for life? What if he refuses to obey?"

"He shall fall ill and wither away like a leaf."

A dreadful silence fell between James and the garden fairies. "If he ever tries to forsake the garden, it shall be his doom. The garden's magic is his breath of life—without it, he cannot survive."

"But how will Father and Ruth ever know this?"

"The truth shall be revealed to them in dreams."

"And what if they doubt?"

"There is no other way."

James lowered his eyes and spoke for the last time: "Tell me, dear fairy... is there no hope? Can such a tragedy be prevented for the poor child?"

"A life for a flower. A flower for a life."

Although he did not understand the meaning of the white fairy's words, he was ready to lay down his life for his garden. It was all meant to be, destined and written in the stars. An ancient pact was made. A pact never to be broken. On that summer night, James became one with the fairies, bound forever to the garden he had cherished above all else. He shut his eyes and faded into the night. But a part of him was reborn in a boy named Henry, born a year later and raised to believe that Thomas was his grandfather.

Yet Thomas could never truly accept the boy. To him, Henry was a tragedy, a living reminder of his son's sacrifice. No one could replace James — no one could fill the void in his heart. Therefore, Thomas resented the garden fairies for their cruel bargain. In his view, his son's sacrifice had brought only sorrow and misfortune upon their once-happy home. He called it the curse of the fairies.

CHAPTER 15

THE CURSE OF THE FAIRIES

Was it truly the curse of the fairies?

On another dreary and rainy afternoon, Ruth, gazing wistfully at the garden, recalled Henry as a little boy.

"Mother, why must I stay here?"

"Because, my sweet boy, you are meant to watch over this garden."

"But I do not want to! I want to see the world…"

"That is nonsense!" replied Thomas harshly. "You shall remain here. And when you are grown, you'll be a gardener, same as your father."

Henry was only five—too young to understand the bitter truth. Even then, Thomas's unkindness toward the boy was unmistakable. Having never acknowledged him as his son, he forbade Ruth from naming him James. Henry and James—two gardeners fated to the same path. Bound forever in a magical prison, left at the mercy of the fairies. One loathed the garden; the other gave his life for it.

"Why do you weep, Ruth?" Isabelle asked. "Is it because of Henry?"

"Why can we not live in peace? What sorrow has befallen us?"

"I have heard that Miss Victoria has had a quarrel with Henry as well."

"It feels as though we are truly cursed," Ruth murmured.

"I cannot believe such nonsense."

"Oh, if only you knew..." replied Ruth in a low voice. Outside, the rain nourished the roses and the garden. Even the heavens seemed to mourn the fate of these unfortunate souls.

"I have often wondered," Isabelle said after a long pause. "Why Thomas forbids Henry from ever leaving this place?"

"Because he's his grandfather, and knows what's best for him."

"He is a cruel and selfish man, that's what he is!"

"He must have his reasons," replied Ruth, turning away to avoid the subject.

It was clear why Thomas acted the way he did. As

he was trying to prevent an inevitable tragedy. And yet, one could not help but wonder: Why fight so hard to keep a boy he so clearly despised? Could it be that, somewhere within that cold heart, was a shred of compassion for Henry?

Even Adam found himself unhappy. For the first time, his daughter had told him, *"I hate you."* Many sleepless nights, and the days seemed endless, unbearable. *"What am I to do?"* he wondered. *"Will she ever forgive me?"*

...

Meanwhile, Victoria was enjoying the rain on her soft skin, her head tilted toward the grey sky as she wept along with it. She felt lonesome, in a world that no longer made sense. Her mind wandered back to that fateful night... when she saw the garden fairies—the very same creatures James had seen fifteen years before. *Garden fairies*, they were called, each one unique, each a living embodiment of a flower. From the very moment Victoria beheld them, she was enchanted—as James had once been. The garden shimmered beneath their ethereal presence. For it was they who breathed life and beauty into the flowers. *"The fairies will help me,"* she thought. *"They are unlike people—they are kind and gentle."* She spoke with such innocence, believing the magical creatures to be incapable of cruelty. Rain drenched her hair, her face, her gown—but the sensation felt almost sacred, calming her troubled soul. Henry, too, was fond of the rain— but for quite different reasons. Whenever it rained, he didn't have to tend the garden. He had grown weary of the gardener's life. He felt like a caged bird; he had wings to fly, but no freedom to buy. Oftentimes, he yearned of running away. And yet, he stayed— for the sake of his mother. *"Why was I born at all?"* A question that haunted him more often than he could admit. He knew nothing of the truth. And if he had known the truth—what then? That secret must remain buried for his own good.

Later, as he lay upon his bed, Ruth came in carrying a plate of biscuits and a glass of milk. "Here, my dear boy... I made them this morning."

"Thank you, Mother," he said, forcing a smile through his heartache.

"What troubles you, my son?" she asked, sitting beside him. "It grieves me to see you so..."

"Do not grieve for me, Mother."

Ruth could no longer restrain her tears. She longed to tell him the truth, but lacked the courage to do so. She hadn't been entirely true to him. How could she explain that he was unlike any other? That he was made of magic and moonlight? That he was, in truth, a prisoner, and always would be?

"Why do you cry?" he asked, gently wiping her tears.

"Oh, I can bear it no longer."

Henry wrapped his arms around her with deep affection. Then he whispered silently to her: "Mother... don't be angry with me... but I have decided to leave this place."

Ruth felt her heart nearly stop, hearing the very words she had prayed never to hear. She touched his face, and through tears, she pleaded: "Don't go, Henry. I beg of you."

He kissed her trembling hands. "I've made up my mind, dearest Mother."

"But why? Where will you go?"

"Anywhere but here."

"You are just a boy..." she whispered, her voice breaking.

"Do you wish me to remain but a wretched

gardener? I am capable of far greater things, Mother."

Ruth could not argue with his dreams and was being unjust, yet his departure would only mean one thing. She said no more and rushed to Thomas. She burst into his room without knocking as he was staring pensively at his fairy pendant.

"Have you no manners, woman?"

"Henry... Henry..." she cried, out of breath.

"What on earth are you saying?"

"He just told me: He means to leave!"

"What say you?" Thomas shouted. "That is out of the question! He cannot leave this place!"

"And how should he know? You must hurry and do something!" Ruth cried, falling to her knees in despair. "Please, I don't want him to... die."

"Hush, woman! Not so loud! He'll do nothing of the sort," he said with absolute certainty, then gave her a helping hand.

"What shall we do?" asked Ruth.

Thomas put the pendant around his neck and left without adding a word. He headed straight to Victoria. Things hadn't been good between them lately, yet she remained his only hope. He knocked on her door, and when she opened it, she looked upon him and wondered: *"What could he possibly want?"*

"May I come in, miss?" he inquired politely.

"You may," she replied, somewhat surprised. Her room was still invaded by flowers. "Did Papa send you?" she asked.

"No. This concerns the boy."

"Henry?"

"He wishes to leave. And only you can prevent him from doing so."

"Why should I?"

"Because you are his friend... are you not?"

"Well, not anymore."

"Would you have him leave?"

Victoria paused briefly, before answering truthfully: "No! I want him to stay."

Thomas felt a wave of relief when he heard those words. He had a strong feeling that her arrival was no coincidence—perhaps she truly was the key to their salvation.

"That is precisely what I hoped to hear," he gave a kind smile.

Victoria was clueless. His manner seemed

somewhat strange and unpredictable. He seemed different—softer, more human.

"And you?" she asked him earnestly. "Do you wish him gone?"

"No," he sighed heavily.

"You are his grandfather, after all."

Thomas was in disbelief. "Who told you that, miss?"

"The garden fairies told me."

"What did you say?" he was shocked. "The garden fairies? They are here? Have you seen them?"

"You've seen them as well?"

Then he swore under his breath: "Damn those fairies!"

"What is it?"

"Pray that the boy stays, miss. This is a grave matter."

After having uttered those words, Thomas faded like the wind. He was in disbelief upon learning that the fairies had indeed returned. He feared they hadn't come back in vain—that they had returned to take more. As if James's life hadn't been enough. Victoria wasted no time and rushed to change her friend's mind. Henry had already packed his suitcase, prepared to leave that very same day. His door was open when she stepped in quietly.

"Is something the matter? What do you want?" he asked when he saw her pale face.

"Don't go!" she said tearfully.

"What did you say?"

"Please, don't leave, Henry. Stay here... with me."

"Who told you I was leaving?"

"It does not matter. Don't go..."

He saw the sadness in her eyes, the sincerity in her voice. Her words moved him more than he expected. "Why would you have me stay?"

"Because... you are my dearest friend. I'll treat you better from now on, I swear it..."

"Your dearest friend? You mean your only friend?" he said with a smirk.

"You restored my smile... remember?" she murmured, wiping away her tears. "You made me believe in true friendship."

Henry was left speechless. They stood in silence, facing one another. He broke the silence at last. "All right, I'll stay—but not for long."

CHAPTER 16

VICTORIA'S MELANCHOLY

Adam had not yet asked his daughter for forgiveness, and their dispute was making him very upset. Consumed by remorse and silent despair, he approached her room, resting his forehead against the door as he exhaled deeply. Little did he know, Victoria was behind him.

"Papa?"

He turned at once and saw her smiling gently. "My sweet girl!" he cried joyfully. Then knelt before her and took her in his arms: "Please forgive me, my darling. I am not a perfect father, and I never meant to cause you pain."

Victoria had a fiery temperament and often let her emotions get the better of her, yet forgiveness was her virtue. "No. Forgive me, Papa!" she whispered, touching his face with her small hands.

"Nonsense... my dear. You are not to blame. It was

I who spoke such cruel words. Say... you forgive me?"

"It's all right, Papa," she said softly, wrapping her arms around him. "I forgive you."

"Bless my soul!" he drew her close. "The thought of you hating me... it was more than I could bear."

"I love you more than anything in the world, Papa. Nothing could ever part me from you." And so they remained, father and daughter, reconciled in each other's arms. Whatever bitterness had come between them faded into insignificance.

...

The next morning, the sky turned grey with dark clouds. The wind howled in all directions, its whistles speaking in foreign tongues. Thomas stepped outside with a frightening look on his face. Though it was past dawn, the sun was nowhere to be seen, as if hiding from whatever was to come.

"I knew it. They're up to something. Curse them!" he muttered to himself. A great fear took over him. The fairies had returned—and their presence was not a good sign. Without wasting another second, he went to find Victoria. He needed to know what the fairies had told her. He found her seated alone in the living room. Luckily for him, no one else was around.

"Good morning, miss," he said with a slight bow.

"Good morning," she replied quietly.

"I trust you slept well."

"Very well, indeed."

"May I speak with you, miss?" He wasted no time. "You spoke of the fairies—that they had revealed something to you. Concerning me."

"Yes, they told me who you truly are."

"Did they speak of anything else?"

"Why such curiosity?" she raised an eyebrow. "Why do you ask about the fairies? Where have you seen them?"

"They appeared to me in a dream."

"For what purpose?"

"I dare not say, miss. It is a matter of secrecy—I am not at liberty to speak of it."

"Well, if you won't share your secret, then I won't share mine," she said with a pout, leaving him quite speechless. Though Thomas's heart couldn't rest— something troubled his soul; In that very moment, a most dreadful thought crossed his mind: *"Could they have returned... for the boy?"*

By afternoon, the dark clouds had dispersed. Adam had started writing again after two years of silence. Something had inspired him, awakening his desire to pick up the pen once more. Victoria entered his study while he was in the midst of shaping his next masterpiece.

"What are you doing, Papa?"

"I am writing."

"Oh! And what is it about?"

"Come closer, my dear," he said with a warm smile. She sat on his lap and glanced at the title written across the page: *Victoria's Melancholy.*

"Papa... are you writing about me?"

"Indeed. Victoria shall be the main character."

"But... why choose my name?"

"Because it is most dear to me. You are my constant inspiration."

"I fear this play will not succeed," she said in a low voice. "because... all that concerns me ends in misfortune."

Adam watched her with deep compassion, brushing the hair from her eyes. "You mustn't speak so, Victoria. You carry more light than you know."

"Papa..."

"Yes, my darling?"

"Don't let Henry leave."

"Why? Where would he go?"

"He wanted to, but I stopped him..."

"And how did you manage that?"

"Strangely enough... he listened to me."

"What reason did he have?"

"I cannot say, Papa."

"And why was I not informed of this?" Adam exclaimed in surprise.

"It was Thomas! He asked me to persuade him."

"Thomas?"

"Yes. Did you know that he is Henry's grandfather?"

"Of course. I presumed you knew as well."

"I did not. Henry never spoke of it."

"Thomas seldom speaks of his past," Adam replied.

"Yet I have heard that his son, presumably, Henry's father, passed on many years ago, under rather mysterious circumstances. But I have no desire to meddle in affairs that do not concern me, nor should you."

Victoria nodded. "Papa, what would you have done, had Henry asked permission to leave?"

"I should have granted it."

"But why?"

"You must not be unjust, Victoria. He is free to pursue his dreams as he sees fit."

"You are right, Papa," she agreed. "He deserves to be happy. And if happiness lies elsewhere, far from here, then I must wish him well."

Victoria regretted having interfered in Henry's decision. She had always taken her father's advice to heart. "*Poor Henry,*" she thought. "*How alike we are. I lost my dear mother, and he lost his father.*"

Later, while searching for him, she ran into Thomas, pacing anxiously in the hall. Recalling the conversation of that very morning, she avoided him and made her way into the garden in hopes of finding Henry. Yet, he was nowhere to be seen. She began calling out, "Henry!"—but no response. She wandered deeper into the garden, but something felt off. The garden seemed to change around her, transforming into a darker and unfamiliar forest. It was no longer a garden. "*Where is this place? Where am I? This is not the garden.*" Victoria was dreadfully frightened and started running, her voice trembling as she shouted: "Henry! Where are you? Answer me!!" But the dark forest was utterly still and lifeless. It felt like a hedge maze with no way out. Suddenly, she lost consciousness and collapsed onto the withered leaves, the world around her fading to black.

"Victoria! Victoria!"

When she opened her eyes, she saw Henry facing her. He had found her unconscious and carried her back inside.

"Where am I?" she spoke with a faint voice.

"Why, you are home!"

"Where were you? I searched for you everywhere..."

"I was in the garden."

"Nonsense! I didn't see you there."

"What happened to you? Why did you faint?"

"I saw a dark forest, where there is no life..." she whispered with a haunted look.

"What are you saying?" Henry shook his head. Shortly after, her father and the others burst into the room, having heard what had happened.

"Victoria!" Adam called. "Are you all right?"

"Yes, Papa."

"And what has occurred?" Thomas turned to Henry.

"I found her senseless in the garden," the boy explained. Adam kissed her gently on the forehead, telling her not to worry. They all assumed her fainting was due to her fragile health, but Victoria knew better. She had seen something no one else could understand. And in her heart, she knew that no one would ever believe her.

CHAPTER 17

FEARS AND SECRETS

Victoria was unwell and bedridden for days. As Isabelle was bringing her tea, Thomas stepped forward and took it from her hands. "I shall see to this myself. Back to the kitchen, girl."

He alone suspected that the fairies had had a hand in Victoria's illness. He could not rest until he uncovered the truth of that fateful night. Knocking lightly at the door, he then entered respectfully.

"Your tea, miss."

"What are you doing here?"

"I came to bring your tea."

"I don't believe you," she said firmly. "You have come to question me again—about the fairies."

"You are quite right," he admitted at last. "But I do so for a very good reason."

"I do not wish to speak to you."

"What if I were to tell you," he said, his voice

softening, "that I am the only soul in this house who believes you?"

"Believes me about what, precisely?"

"About what happened three days ago," he answered, raising an eyebrow.

She fell silent. After all, he was telling the truth— only he knew of the fairies' existence. She had no choice but to confess. "Very well then," she sighed at last. "What is it you wish to know?"

"All of it."

"But first... I should like my tea."

"As you wish, miss." Thomas poured the tea into her cup. He stood respectfully aside, awaiting her word.

"When I saw them that night... I was the happiest girl in the world. They were the most enchanting creatures in the garden. They showed me how they bestow beauty upon the world through their wondrous gifts." she paused.

"Did they say nothing further?"

"That I can't remember..."

"Oh, but you must! This may be of the utmost importance."

"And why should that be?"

"Because it concerns Henry."

"Henry?" she was utterly surprised. "What could they possibly have to do with him? Do you mean, perhaps, because he is the gardener?"

"Or better said... their prisoner," Thomas thought silently. Before Victoria could speak another word, a sudden knock interrupted them. Before leaving, he advised her not to speak to anyone about the fairies. "You must speak of this to no one," he added. "Not even to your father. For your sake, and ours, this must remain a secret."

Moments later, Ruth entered the room and was surprised to see him leaving with no explanation at all.

"Are you feeling any better, miss?"

"Yes."

"And what, may I ask, was Thomas doing here?"

"Oh, nothing of importance."

"Oh... I see," said Ruth, asking no more.

...

Once Victoria regained her strength, her father decided to take her with him to London. He had received an invitation to a formal engagement and believed it might lift her spirits. Yet she didn't seem interested. "You go, Papa. I would rather stay."

Adam, however, had no intention of leaving her alone again. Not after everything that had happened. "No, darling," he said firmly. "You must come with me this time. We shan't be gone long."

"I'd like to stay!"

"Come now, Victoria. Not so very long ago, you beseeched me to take you with me. What has changed so suddenly?"

"People change, Papa."

Her response unsettled him. He knew his daughter well, and the light in her once-bright eyes was dimming.

"You are keeping something from me, are you not?"

Victoria turned from him, concealing fears and secrets far too heavy for a twelve-year-old. Yet she also understood her father's scepticism toward fairy tales.

"No... I am not hiding anything," she denied.

Before leaving her room, Adam added: "Very well. I shall depart in two days' time. You have until then to make a choice."

She gave no reply. Her thoughts no longer lingered on London or her former life. Her mind belonged solely to the garden fairies. In truth, she hardly slept at night, hoping and longing for their return.

Later that day, she rose from her bed, making her way to the place where she always met her dear companion. She called his name out loudly, and when Henry turned, he saw her running toward him.

"Are you feeling better now?"

"I am, thank God!"

"I am pleased to hear that," he said with a gentle smile.

"Thank you, Henry..." she said unexpectedly.

"For what?"

"For remaining by my side while I was ill."

"We are friends, are we not?"

She hugged him tightly and, with teary eyes, whispered, "I don't know what I would have done without you."

Henry said nothing. He could not speak. He pulled his cap low over his teary eyes, embarrassed by his sudden fragility. Victoria had only ever embraced three people in her life: her mother, her father, and her beloved friend, whom she cherished like a brother. Fate, it seemed, had drawn them together for reasons neither of them can fathom. The sun had begun to set. Golden leaves falling one by one, painting the garden in warm, reddish tones. Henry was gathering them quietly, and Victoria helped.

"Oh, the poor leaves," she murmured sadly. "Look how they've withered!"

"It is autumn," he replied, "The season when all things begin to fade."

"I wish the flowers would never die."

"And... I cannot wait for winter."

"Are you? But why?"

"Because in winter, I don't have to work in the garden."

"If you so dislike it, why not quit?"

"I cannot," he said, as he gathered the fallen leaves.

"Says who?"

"My mother and Thomas. I was meant to be a gardener from the day I was born. They call it my father's legacy. Utter rubbish!"

"And what do you believe?"

"I believe it to be a curse," he said quietly. "There is something I have not told you... Thomas is —"

"Your grandfather," she replied quickly.

"How do you know?"

"He told me so himself."

"He did? That is unbelievable! He keeps it a secret from everyone."

"Why would he?"

"He is ashamed of me. Does your father know?"

She nodded. "He does."

There was a brief silence between them. Then she added: "Papa is going to London."

"Is he? When?"

"In two days. He insists I go with him."

"And... have you made your decision?"

"I am still considering."

His expression shifted, and though he did his best to conceal it, the sadness in his eyes betrayed him.

"I envy you—London must be quite wonderful."

"Not really. It is crowded and terribly loud. I prefer it here."

"I shall miss you."

"I'm not going forever," she laughed gently. "I'll be back before you know it."

"I have a strange feeling."

"What sort of feeling?"

"I cannot say. It came upon me so suddenly."

"Do tell!"

"I fear... I may never see you again."

A dreadful silence fell upon them as night approached, until Victoria spoke at last. "If that's truly how you feel, then I'll stay."

"Think nothing of it."

"I, Victoria Erin Flynn," she declared, placing her hand over her heart as though making the most sacred of vows, "do promise to stay here, with my cowardly friend, Henry Green."

"Don't be silly!" he chuckled, finding her words amusing.

"It's all right. I had no real intention of going."

"Don't stay because of me, Victoria."

"Do you remember when you stayed for my sake?"

"Yes, of course."

"Well then... I think we are now even."

CHAPTER 18

OCTOBER

Two days later, Adam departed on his journey—this time without Victoria. He had entrusted Thomas with the task of watching over her, observing her every movement, for he feared for her well-being. Since the recent unsettling events, Thomas had become more vigilant than ever. There were nights when he did not sleep, pacing the halls like a restless spirit. He remained alert day and night, for he had never trusted the fairies or their enchantments. In his eyes, they were no fragile, godlike creatures, but sinister and deceitful spirits. Yet it was not only the fairies who haunted his sleepless nights; his conscience also kept him awake. The guilt had begun to torment him. The memory of James lay heavy upon his mind. In both appearance and defiant nature, Henry was the image of his late son. After all, the boy was his son's reincarnation. Exhausted and tormented by recent events, he confided in Ruth regarding the fairies.

"They have returned? How dreadful!" she cried.

"Hush, not so loud!" Thomas muttered.

"What is it they want now? Have they not already taken enough?"

"It appears they want more."

"I fear they have come for my son."

"Perhaps not," he said, shaking his head. "This time... they have come for the girl."

"But why her?" she whispered.

"I haven't the slightest idea. They are luring her with magic spells and illusions."

"Oh, my poor, dear girl! Heaven forbid—it cannot be what I suspect."

"That can't be! My son has already paid the price— Will this dreadful nightmare never end? I had truly believed we were rid of them."

"You fear for Henry, do you not?" she asked, watching him closely. He gave no reply. Instead, he turned and walked away. Yet Ruth understood. He did care for the boy, there was a trace of compassion in him still, though his pride was stronger.

...

It was the 5th of October 1855, Victoria's 13th birthday was but seven days ahead. Only her father knew of this. He had sent her a note, promising his return in due course.

"What shall become of the garden?" Victoria wondered in a sad voice. The once vibrant garden had begun to wither and fade beneath the breath of October.

"Nothing at all," Henry replied. "You've no idea how lovely it looks in winter—when all is covered in snow."

"And why does that please you?" she frowned. "The flowers will die."

"They'll bloom again in spring."

"But I wish... I wish the garden would bloom forever."

Henry paused, then said something to lift her spirit. "Come now! Shall we toss the leaves into the air?" Victoria nodded in agreement, and they plunged into the pile of autumn leaves as if diving into a sea of colour. The leaves soared like butterflies, then drifted back gently over their heads. Victoria's face beamed with joy whenever she was in Henry's company. That enchanted garden had become the cradle of their friendship.

As dusk fell upon them, they began to tidy the mess they had made. "Look at my hands and my dress — they are utterly filthy!" she complained.

"Oh! I had quite forgotten — you're a princess," he said with a silly smirk.

"Henry... my birthday..." she murmured.

"What?"

"My birthday is seven days ahead," she finally told him.

"Is that so? Why did you not tell me before?"

"Never mind. It is of no importance."

"Whatever makes you say such a thing?"

"I do not wish to grow older," she replied. "But you do... don't you, Henry? To become a man?"

"What sort of question is that? Of course I do!"

Just then, Isabelle called out from the house — supper was ready. The children were both starving. As Victoria took her seat, she called: "Come now, Henry! You must be quite famished."

But Ruth gently stepped in. "Henry's supper is served in the kitchen, miss."

"All right then..." said the boy, glancing at his mother.

"Henry, wait!" Victoria exclaimed. "You can sit with me. I insist!"

"But he is a servant, miss!" Isabelle meddled.

"Nonsense!" she replied firmly. "He is no servant—he is my friend."

Fortunately, Thomas was not home; he would never have given his approval. The order of the household had been disturbed.

"Did you see how she insisted Henry dine with her?" Isabelle whispered. "Thank the heavens the old man was not here to see it."

"Oh, hush!" Ruth sighed after a long, tiring day.

...

By midnight, all were asleep—except Thomas. He wasn't home and had yet to return. The night was wistfully quiet. From the garden came a haunting melody, soft and alluring. Like a whispered invitation, it found its way into Victoria's ears. She rose from her bed, wandering barefoot through the cold, drawn by the spell of music. When Thomas at last returned, a faint sound caught his ear. There, in the garden, he beheld Victoria, utterly bewitched. He called her name once, twice—but there was no answer. Then lifted her gently into his arms and carried her back into the house. As he laid her down upon her bed, he muttered under his breath, "Curse you, fairies!!"

CHAPTER 19

THE BOY AND THE FAIRY GARDEN

Henry was a young gardener, and his life had begun with a lie. Poor boy—his dreams, so full of brightness, were doomed to tragedy. He longed for distant lands, foreign skies and grand adventures. Yet in a world as cold and merciless as this, such dreams perish quietly, day by day.

"Who is it?"

"It is me—Victoria!"

"One moment, if you please!"

The door was locked. Victoria was standing outside his bedroom, wondering why he was taking so long. She leaned closer and heard the clink of a hammer.

"How much longer, Henry?"

"Almost done!"

"What on earth are you doing in there?"

"I cannot say."

"Why not?"

"Because it is a secret."

She sighed, her patience already wearing thin. Just as she was about to leave, the door creaked open.

"Here I am!" he grinned.

"What is it you're working on?" she asked, folding her arms.

"Oh—nothing at all," he replied as he began to whistle.

"Don't lie to me. You spoke of a secret."

"I'm making something. For you."

"For me?" she blushed. "Whatever for?"

"I told you—it's a secret. But you shall know soon enough."

Like an impatient child, her curiosity refused to be quieted. "Tell me this instant, Henry."

"I cannot," he said with a soft chuckle. With that, Henry stepped outside—the day was not yet over, and there was much to be done in the garden. From an upper window, Thomas watched him quietly. He remembered the dream. That ill-fated night when the fairies came to him and spoke of a boy and the fairy garden. A child who would one day take James's place and devote his life to their sacred garden. He recalled each word—and that memory only deepened his quiet hatred for them.

"Your son, James, was sacrificed for the sake of our garden. And so, a part of him shall be reborn as a boy. Created by our ancient magic, he shall serve us faithfully and tend to our flowers for the entirety of his days. We shall grant him breath; we shall grant him life—but freedom shall be denied. Yet, he may dream... for dreams are not forbidden. The boy shall live and die as any mortal. But his life belongs to the fairy garden. Here lies both his beginning and his end. Beware: the desire to forsake this garden shall bring him endless sorrow. And his departure... shall bring him death."

That bitter warning had tormented him for fifteen years. Henry was born into this world under a dreadful curse, marked by the fairies—spiteful creatures thirsting for human sacrifice. Even Ruth had been told why she was chosen to bear the accursed child: for her virtues, such as honesty and loyalty. But what good had the fairies ever brought, aside from the garden's beguiling beauty? They demanded James's life, and took it without a shred of remorse. They had promised his garden to bloom eternally, yet it did not. Their hunger knows no bounds, and they will not cease until all is theirs. Man—a fragile, powerless creation of God—how might he withstand such ancient and ruthless beings? How will Henry respond once the truth comes forth? Who will comfort him? And will he submit to his accursed fate?

"That's enough for today, boy!" Thomas said before walking away. Victoria observed the sadness that lingered in Henry's eyes. "Why do you not talk to him?"

"There's no use in talking to him," he replied.

"Are you sure?"

"I despise him."

"I find that hard to believe. He is your grandfather."

"So what?"

"Family is to be respected. Papa often says so."

"He has not earned my respect," Henry said, his voice unsteady. "He's been nothing but unkind to me."

"Have you ever asked him why?"

"He gives no reason—only ever speaks of my father, says I'll never be like him, as though he blames me for something."

...

Henry was once again looking forward to Victoria's birthday. He had carefully crafted a symbolic gift from wood—with a personal meaning. It hadn't been long since she had moved there, yet to him, it felt as if he'd known her a lifetime. At first, the transition from city life to the countryside proved challenging for Victoria. But as time often does, it healed all wounds. She had changed. Gone was the timid, unsmiling girl who preferred only the company of herself. Now she was full of light and spirit. Her imagination had always been her refuge—a safe haven built upon dreams. Beneath her quiet strength lay a wound no child should ever bear: the loss of a mother. Days turned to weeks, weeks to months, and months to years of silent agony. Her mother never returned. Still, Victoria clung to the hope of miracles, firmly believing that, one day, she might come back. For nearly two years, she had not uttered a single word—not from an illness, but from a broken heart. Now, at last, she had found peace. Surrounded by kind, trustworthy people who truly saw her for who she is.

She was seated upon a chair, placing roses into a

glass vase. The window was open, and a soft breeze drifted in, brushing gently through her golden hair. Suddenly, a thought crossed her mind: *"I wish Henry were my brother."* A lovely wish, indeed. For the first time in her life, she yearned for a brother. In her imagination, she beheld a future—Adam, Henry, and herself, in a family portrait. *"When Papa returns, I'll ask him to adopt Henry."* Such innocent, child-like thoughts—moments where all seemed possible, and nothing was beyond reach.

"Victoria! Victoria!"

"You have returned? Wait, I'm coming..."

"Come to us, Victoria. Come!"

All of a sudden, a hand touched her shoulder and pulled her from the dream. She opened her eyes to find Ruth standing before her.

"Are you all right, miss?"

"What... what happened?" she murmured, realising she had fallen asleep in a chair.

"You were talking in your sleep, dear."

"I was dreaming..."

"Forgive me for waking you, but you gave me quite a fright."

"It's all right, Ruth," said Victoria kindly.

"Come, child," Ruth smiled. "Let me get you to your bed now."

Ruth's hand, as it softly stroked her hair, became — if only for a moment—her mother's hand. Victoria imagined her mother tucking her in, smiling with the tenderness of an angel. In Ruth's arms, she found comfort, and the bad dreams stayed away. The fairies troubled her no more. She slept in quiet peace, wishing morning might never break—for sleep was far too sweet to end.

...

The following day dawned with heartbreak and sorrow. Someone lay on the cold floor, gasping for air, shirt soaked in sweat, and their body burning with fever. That someone was Henry—struck down in the dead of night by some strange illness. The bedroom door was locked. No one heard his suffering, nor could he call out for help. What had befallen him? Was this the fairies' curse? Thomas noticed his absence almost at once—since Henry was always early. Concerned, he made his way to the boy's room and knocked once. Then Twice. A third time, with more force. Still no reply. After that, he went to Ruth and asked if she had seen him. She shook her head and told him he hadn't come out at all. Thankfully, he fetched the spare key. A sudden dread crept over him. He unlocked the door, and what he saw made his blood run cold. He found the boy on the floor, deathly pale and unresponsive. "Good heavens, Henry!" he exclaimed, hurrying to his side. "What on earth has happened to you?" Thomas laid him on the bed with care. As soon as she was told, Ruth rushed in with a bowl of ice-cold water. "Oh, what has come over my poor boy?" she cried, as she ran to his bedside. Then Thomas swiftly pressed a damp cloth to his forehead.

"Henry? Henry, answer me..." his mother pleaded. Yet there came no response. The nameless illness had seized him utterly, paralyzing both mind and body. Her mournful cries woke little Victoria from her sleep. Thomas gently guided Ruth out of the room, struggling to keep her calm. The dreadful thought of losing Henry weighed heavily upon his heart. "Don't die on me now!" he whispered over and over. "Do you hear me, boy?"

"What's happened to Henry?" a soft voice interrupted. He turned his head to find Victoria standing in the doorway, still in her nightgown.

Upon seeing her friend's condition, she let out a cry and rushed to his side.

"Is he dead? No, no—Henry, Henry!" she sobbed, clutching his hand. Thomas turned his tearful eyes away. All feared the worst—that he was beyond reach. The beating of his heart was slow and faint; though he seemed to hear their voices, he could not respond. His mind and soul were trapped in another dimension. As Victoria wept, a single tear landed upon Henry's hand—and then, miraculously, his fingers moved. Thomas rushed to his side, pressing his ear to his chest. Then he touched the boy's forehead, checking if the fever had gone down.

"He lives," he murmured, "but his pulse is faint."

"What does this mean?" she asked, her voice trembling. "Is Henry in danger?"

"At any moment... we may lose him."

"Hush... do not say such words!" Her voice hardened, and her blue eyes grew wide with fear. "You wish him dead. You hate him! You hate him!" Victoria was angry, unaware of her own words, overcome by sorrow and pain. The mere thought of losing Henry was more than she could bear. "Get out! I order you! Be gone!" she kept demanding.

Her words, though harsh, carried a bitter truth. Thomas had been cruel—unjust to the boy, blaming him for what had befallen James. He had no right to be near him in such a time, much less to mourn him.

"You hate him... you are a cruel man!"

At last, Thomas spoke, his voice low and steady. "I do not hate him, because he is..."

"Because what?"

"Because... Henry is my son."

CHAPTER 20

A LIFE FOR A FLOWER
A FLOWER FOR A LIFE

"Because... Henry is my son."

The words that fell from Thomas's lips were, to Victoria, quite beyond comprehension. Yet he could no longer remain silent about the misfortune that had haunted him through the years. *"No more lies,"* he told himself. No soul shall find peace whilst concealing the truth.

"I have not been entirely truthful," he confessed as he sighed. "No more secrets, you deserve to know the truth."

"What truth?"

"The truth about Henry—and the fairy garden."

And so, Thomas unburdened his soul. He spoke of James—his sacrifice—the true circumstances of Henry's birth, and the dreadful curse cast by the fairies. He spared no detail, unaware that Henry had been listening from the shadows all along. It was in that moment that the boy's world shattered. His very existence had been a lie. They had concealed the truth from him, hoping to shield him from grief and despair.

"Why did you keep it from him?" Victoria asked.

"I was afraid, for he would have disregarded the fairies, even if it meant losing his very life," Thomas replied, his voice heavy with sorrow.

Victoria turned to Henry with a look of aching tenderness. "You deserve none of this burden," she whispered. Her sweet and gentle words reached deep into Henry's fragile heart. And in that stillness, he wept—silently—for the sorrowful truth. Nothing weighed heavier upon his spirit than the cruel revelation. His heart found no solace; no remedy could be found for his misery. The fairies had not granted him life—they had stolen it and deprived him of the most precious gift of all: his freedom. He was their prisoner—bound for all eternity. Death was his only wish. *"I wish to die!"* he thought to himself. *"Who am I? This is not me. My entire life is a lie."*

In that hour of despair, the darkness that had

consumed his world began to lift like a fading mist, overcome by a powerful light. A divine glow, reflecting the image of a small girl with fairy wings— her face radiant as the moon. She had conquered pain and solitude. And that girl... was Victoria.

"Come with me, Henry," she spoke, extending her hand.

"I don't want to live..." Henry answered in despair.

"Who shall watch over me when you're gone?"

And then he remembered—the promise he had made to her. He had vowed to always protect her.

"I must return... she needs me..."

"What do you say then?"

"I... I..."

"Speak, Henry. Have no fear."

"I wish to live. I wish to see the world."

Then, he awoke from the dreadful nightmare that had consumed him, imprisoning his soul. It was Victoria's light, that brought him to life. She had rescued her dearest friend.

"Oh, Henry! You're back!" she cried out with joy, throwing her arms around him, forgetting for a moment how fragile he still was.

"It was you, Victoria. You were the light that brought me

back," he thought silently.

Then, Ruth and Isabelle entered, crying tears of joy. Thomas, meanwhile, slipped away in silence, like a shadow.

"If you please, I should like a moment alone with Victoria," he said all of a sudden.

"Of course," Ruth replied, gently drawing Isabelle away. Henry rose slowly from his bed, sighing deeply before turning to her. "I know the truth."

"The truth?" her voice trembling.

"The truth about me."

"Oh, Henry..."

"Let it be known to all that I will do as I please with my life."

"By all means, it is your life."

"Indeed. It is mine, and mine alone."

"But should you leave, then—"

"So be it! I fear neither fairies nor death."

"They're real... I have seen them with my own eyes."

"I refuse to be their prisoner. One day, I shall leave this accursed place—far from all... far from Thomas."

"Far from me..." she murmured silently. "But what

of Thomas? Will you ever forgive him? After all, he is your father."

"My father?" he replied with a smirk. "He is James's father, not mine. I shall not spend my life in his shadow—nor live at the mercy of the fairies."

All of a sudden, she interrupted him with a gentle request. "Henry," she paused, "Would you like to be my brother?"

The young gardener let his body fall freely upon his bed and burst into laughter. Her words struck him as both absurd and wonderfully sweet. Soon, Victoria joined in his laughter.

...

Several days later, one day before Victoria's birthday, Adam returned from London. He came bearing gifts for his little girl, his heart full of delight. Henry had confided in Ruth the secret he had uncovered, while Thomas now found himself struggling to face him, after all that had come to pass. So, he maintained his distance.

Victoria sat alone in the garden, her thoughts drifting back to the day she first arrived at the house and the many events that had since unfolded. She closed her eyes and took a deep breath, sensing that something was missing. After a while, her father approached quietly, surprising her. "What is this little bird doing here, all alone?"

"Papa!"

"Oh, my sweet Victoria!" Adam said, drawing her into a tender embrace.

"I've missed you!"

"And I you, my love. But tell me, why do you sit here, so lost in thought?"

"I was thinking of the lovely times we have spent together."

"This is only the beginning. You've got so much ahead of you."

"Papa..."

"Yes, my darling?"

"I feel truly blessed to be your daughter. I love you with all my heart."

They remained locked in each other's embrace, as though it were their last, until dusk gently fell upon the garden.

...

That evening, the sky was clearer than ever before, and the moon shone twice as bright. The stars of the night adorned the heavens, their shimmering light dancing across the sky. In the heart of the enchanted garden, little Victoria sat quietly, awaiting the return of her fairies. She wished with all her heart that they would come again. By this time, she had come to understand their true nature—they were not so virtuous, as she had once believed. The gentle, kind-hearted fairies existed only within fairy tales, and not within the garden of her home. And they finally answered her call, gathering around her as they appeared one by one.

"Where have you been?" Victoria asked softly.

"We are here now," the fairies spoke at last.

"Why have you done this to Henry?"

"Because he was disobedient," they replied coldly.

"How cruel you are..." she whispered, suddenly heartbroken.

"We take life, but in exchange, we offer something else."

"In exchange for what? You have condemned him for all eternity!"

"He was forged by our magic. He is ours, and bound to obey."

"He is just a boy!"

"If Henry forsakes us, his due is death."

"Show mercy! What purpose does this cruelty serve?"

"A life for a flower. A flower for a life," spoke the garden fairies all together.

Victoria fell to her knees. Feeling utterly helpless and powerless before their magic. Her blue eyes filled with tears as she thought of her father, Henry, and the others—realizing she could save none of them. In that moment of despair, a gentle hand softly caressed her hair. She raised her head to behold the most beautiful and sacred of beings— her mother, Avelina. She appeared to her as a fairy.

"Mama... is it truly you?"

"Yes, my darling, it is I—your mother."

"Where have you been all this time? I have waited so long."

"I have always been here," she said, pointing tenderly, "within your heart."

"Tell me—why me?"

"Because you are the chosen one."

"The chosen one?"

"Indeed. It is your destiny to break the curse of the fairies once and for all."

"What?"

"My dear Victoria," her mother spoke softly, "I am half human, half fairy—and half-fairies do not live long. You, my child, were born for a purpose: to deliver all those condemned by the fairies' curse." Victoria listened closely, hardly believing her ears. "When the fairies' curse is broken, those afflicted shall be freed, and no more human sacrifices shall be required. This curse was an ancient pact between mankind and the fairy folk, made many centuries past. Yet, when the farmers, in their desperation, beseeched the fairies to bless their fields with fertility and abundance, the fairies demanded a life in exchange. '*A life for a flower. A flower for a life.*' And thus began *the curse of the fairies*, and it is you who must bring an end to this ancient bargain. You must prepare yourself, for your time has come."

"But what am I to do?"

"You were born for this purpose," Avelina replied.

"Why did you leave without a farewell, Mama?" Victoria said through tears.

"I never truly left your side."

"Will we be together now, forever?"

"Forever, my little one."

Those were Avelina's final words before she faded

into the eternal light. Victoria knew her mother now lived somewhere among the flowers in the garden. She wiped away her tears and embraced her destiny. "I promise, Mama! I will save Henry—and all those who have suffered beneath this curse."

"And... what is your final decision?" the fairies inquired at last.

"Should the curse be broken, what is to become of Henry?"

"He shall be released from us."

"Is there hope for his happiness?"

"That, dear child, depends upon him," the garden fairies replied.

"So... he—?"

"He shall be free."

Victoria sighed with relief, knowing deep within her heart that she was doing the right thing. The time had come to prove her love and devotion to those she cherished most dearly. Without a second thought, she took a deep breath, lifted her eyes toward the heavens, and, more certain than ever, declared, "I am ready."

The fairies joined hands around her, forming a glowing circle with Victoria in the middle. As they began their magical ritual, she closed her eyes and spoke in their ancient tongue:

"Darkness, light, sky, earth, sun, moon, stars, planets, water, air, fire, humans, fairies, beasts, nature, flowers, love, hatred, blessing, curse, courage, fear, faith, doubt, hope, despair, joy, suffering, pain, healing, tears, smiles, friendship, family... life and death."

And just like that... Victoria and the garden fairies vanished—like a flash of light across the night sky. That was the moment in which she fulfilled her destiny. She gave her life for Henry—just as James had, fifteen years before. She laid down her life to save another. Her sacrifice was far greater. This time, she broke the ancient curse, forevermore.

...

It was the night when a single star faded from the sky—so the others might shine a little brighter. The moon's silver light streamed softly through Victoria's window, in a room that had fallen into a haunting silence. Her bed lay cold and empty. Her gowns will remain untouched, and her shoes will never walk again. Who could have foreseen that an ordinary night would become a night of sacrifice? The night upon which Victoria wrote the final chapter of her life. The night when all her dreams came to an end. Before she departed for good, one person lingered in her thoughts: Adam. Her final wish was for her father to live on—to find solace, and one day, perhaps, have a new family. That very night, her spirit appeared to him in a dream. *"Come to the garden, Papa…"* That tender voice woke Adam from his sleep. He gazed out the window—but saw nothing. He walked to her room; it was empty. That day was special—it marked her birthday. The day she would have turned thirteen.

Henry was carefully putting the finishing touches on her birthday gift. He had carved a wooden figure of Victoria—complete with fairy wings and a crown of flowers resting upon her head. *"She will be delighted to see this,"* he thought, smiling to himself. Upon stepping into the garden, he could hardly believe his eyes. Though it was the middle of October, the garden was green and in full bloom. The withered leaves had vanished, replaced by vibrant blossoms. The garden was lovelier than he remembered. Suddenly, the wooden figure slipped from his hand when his eyes fell upon something most extraordinary. There, at the heart of the garden, stood a giant red flower—nearly half his height. It was like no flower he had ever beheld: petals soft as the finest silk, in the likeness of a rose. As he drew near, a familiar scent filled his lungs— the scent of Victoria herself. For that flower... was Victoria. Unlike James, she had returned as an eternal flower. A living blossom born of fairy magic. One that would never wither nor fade. She had become a garden flower, to remain close to those she cherished. Kneeling before her, Henry placed the wooden figure beside the flower. The pain in his chest tightened, but so did the warmth in his heart. He understood at last: Victoria would never return as the girl he had known, yet was still amongst them. All understood the necessity of her sacrifice— except Adam, who could not bring himself to accept it. He recalled Avelina's words: *"Victoria was born for a purpose. When she departs, know that it shall be for the good of all."* Words so painful—unthinkable for a father—yet they had become a bitter truth. And somehow, she seemed nearer to him now than ever before. Victoria had transformed into a triumphant and magical flower—one that blooms in every season. Not a day went by without Adam hearing her voice. And one such day, that voice guided him to a small wooden box. Within it, he found a golden pendant—round in shape, engraved with the image of a flower, and bearing a message. With trembling hands and eyes clouded with tears, he read the inscription aloud: *"I AM ALWAYS HERE."* The very same words marked upon Thomas's pendant. A gift from the fairies—bestowed upon the families of the Chosen people. A token of gratitude. A symbol of sacrifice. Adam wept quietly, smiling through his grief, as the tears of a brokenhearted father fell upon the pendant. "Come back to me, Victoria," he whispered.

...

Ten years had come and gone, and their worlds had changed. Henry and Thomas had at last been reconciled. Their bond, as father and son, had grown stronger with the passing of time. Adam had long since returned to London, never to set foot again in the house that had brought him nothing but misery. His final play—*Victoria's Melancholy*—remained unfinished, left abandoned like the dreams he once held dear. In time, he remarried but had no children.

Henry was now a grown man. For a decade, he had tended faithfully to Victoria's flower. It was the least he could do; he owed her his very life. Though nothing held him back, he had never once left the house because of her. However, Thomas and Ruth had persuaded him to pursue his dream, for it was one of Victoria's dearest wishes—that her beloved friend might live free. That, indeed, had been the purpose of her sacrifice: to grant him the life he had long desired. Before setting forth on his journey, ready to begin a new chapter of adventures, Henry wandered once more into the garden. No longer known as the Fairy Garden, but Victoria's Garden. Amidst that place, rich with blossoms and memories, he knelt before her everblooming flower and gently placed a crown of lilies beside her wooden figure. Rising slowly with a warm smile, Henry Green whispered: "Farewell, my fairy."

A Life for a Flower.
A Flower for a Life.

ABOUT THE AUTHOR

I wrote The Fairy Garden in 2011 and named the main character after my mother, who also shares a deep love for flowers. This story is close to my heart, and I hope you enjoyed reading it as much as I enjoyed writing it.

— *Diana Nokaj*

Diana Nokaj was born on May 17th, 1990 in Kosovo. Her fascination with myths and fairy tales inspired her to start writing from a young age. A dreamer at heart, she loves books, nature, castles, and all things medieval fantasy. *The Fairy Garden* is her first published novel, following her poetry collection *Melancholia*. When she's not writing, Diana enjoys reading, drawing, traveling, and spending time with family and friends.

Printed in Dunstable, United Kingdom